The Children of the Earth That Was

by

C.R. Endacott

The Children of the Earth That Was, by C.R. Endacott

Published by World's End Book Publishing
(Previously known as: Endacott and Woolf Book Publishing)
www.fictionbooks.ca

First publication 06-05-2022

ISBN Paperback: 978-1-7753545-1-2

ISBN Hardcover: 978-1-7753545-6-7
Library and Archives Canada

Book Design by World's End Book Publishing

Manufactured in Canada.
Manufactured in the United States of America.

The Children of the Earth That Was

by

C.R. Endacott

Author's Note

As a Caucasian of European descent, I am fully aware of the privilege my heritage has given me.

I did not intend to make this work a discussion about the English language or its privilege over other languages, as in this book, the subservient humans speak English, and the ruling aliens' language is foreign and unrecognizable.

The irony, of course, is that many European nations colonized other nations, perceiving the indigenous peoples as savage. In this case, the aliens could be analogous to European colonizers and the humans as people violated for the sake of another group's colonial ambitions and dominance.

The dominant themes of this story reflect dislocation, colonization, identity, and dominance; also common in other postcolonial books.

The not-so-subtle allegorical significance of the work is an attempt to consider our capacity as humans to take the lives of sentient beings we consider inferior and consume their flesh for food. Though I do not adhere to strict vegetarianism myself, I am deeply concerned about the humane treatment of all life, especially regarding meat processing plants and the sheer number of lives taken to feed our ever-growing population.

Bovines are sentient beings.
Bovines have complex societal systems.
Bovines have complex long-term and
working memory systems.
Bovines have emotions and
emotional responses to stimuli.
Bovines have personalities
such as shyness and gregariousness.
And over 800,000 of them are killed every day.[1]

---

1 Bekoff, Marc. "Cows: Science Shows They're Bright and Emotional Individuals." *Psychology Today*, Sussex Publishers, 2 Nov. 2017, https://www.psychologytoday.com/ca/blog/animal-emotions/201711/cows-science-shows-theyre-bright-and-emotional-individuals

Prologue

Prologue

Messia's belly was fully extended in pregnancy. All the other women in her corral were also late-term pregnancies. A few of the women had already gone into contractions.

She glanced around the corral and counted five Reaper-bots assisting women giving birth. The Overseers never came in to help with this part. It was left totally up to the droids.

Her entire life was spent with this herd. And now she was almost one hundred and ninety seasons. This would be the last child she birthed. Her last out of ten. She considered herself lucky because most women gave birth to only six or seven, and then they went peacefully because their work was done.

The first contractions hit her, and she grunted in pain. But they were fleeting. The labor would be worse before the night was through. One of the Reaper-bots heard her and came over. She lay down on her back, as was expected, and it examined her with a red electronic eye.

A woman named Trini screamed next to her. Her contractions were already steady and coming minutes apart.

The droid left her and went to the other woman. But Messia stayed on the floor. Her brown curly hair was drenched with sweat. Her mind wandered as she counted the seconds between contractions.

The corrals were all she knew. But she had also inadvertently learned a secret. The Overseers, sometimes, would move heifers from one corral to another, and as fate would have it, she was placed in a corral with her own mother. Messia had been about eighty seasons, and her mother one hundred and fifty. The only reason they realized they were blood-related was because they looked so much alike. The same icy eyes, the same curly brown hair, the same body type and build. Her mother's name was Bia.

The Overseers must have lost track; otherwise, they would never have allowed it to happen. They were careful to make sure women who were related always remained separated. But this one time, this one mistake gave Messia the opportunity to ask questions.

She learned that Bia used to live outside the corrals, in a forest free from the Overseers. But one day, she was captured while out foraging for food. She had left a younger sister hidden in the forest, and she never knew what came of her.

Bia told Messia many things about the world. But not things about the Overseers. She knew very little about them, only that if they came near, you had to hide. But it gave Messia hope that there were free people still living outside the corrals.

Another contraction rocked her body, and she gritted her teeth and tried to breathe through the agony, as she had been taught. They were coming closer together now, and once again, the Reaper-bot checked on her. Trini was in the final stages of childbirth, but Messia ignored her now.

"It's coming!" Messia said, her voice pressed and firm. "The child is coming!"

The Reaper-bot responded to her sounds and reached its metallic hand between her legs to help guide the birth. There was no encouragement from the droid; it just waited for the baby's head to crown.

It happened quickly this time. Messia felt the baby's head, and then the cold fingers of the droid's metallic hand entered inside of her and pulled the baby out. It was almost as painful as the contractions, and she gritted her teeth again.

The Reaper-bot cut the umbilical cord. It gave the baby several smacks on the back until it started to cry, and then it placed the baby in her arms before moving to tend to another woman.

Messia looked down at the baby. It was a girl. She had a full head of brown frizzy hair. Most of her children were born with hair. But all of her other children had been males.

She gently stroked the baby girl's head. "You are my last. Your name is Zee. Beautiful Zee."

The baby cried still. Messia lifted her top and exposed her nipple and brushed it along Zee's bottom lip. The baby latched on almost instantly and started sucking.

"Good girl! Strong girl!" she murmured with a smile. It felt like her nipple was being sucked down the baby's throat. "You're a very strong one."

She hummed to herself. "You will learn many things. We have only twelve seasons together before they take you away. But I will teach you to call all women Mother. I will teach you to be strong, to ask questions, and to not be satisfied with life in a corral. And I will pray that you escape this prison and live like a free one."

Messia closed her eyes. She would never see this one grow up, but she felt hope for the future for the second time in her life. This girl would change everything.

Part 1

The White Domes

Chapter 1

ξ

The Barn

I had never actually seen a dead body. Her gaunt skin looked leathery and stretched over her bones. Her eyes were dark, with black circles around them.

At first, the other women stopped by to gawk at the dead woman, partly because none of us actually looked like her. I know I didn't. My skin was a nice pink and there was meat and muscle under it. When I pinched the skin on the back of my hand, it bounced back into place instantly.

"Back away," a woman's voice commanded. Deborah, our leader, our teacher. She was older than us, like all our teachers had been. But her tone was always so stern. Women in our corral whispered that the teachers weren't supposed to be so disagreeable, and that Deborah was the exception, not the rule. Her hair was wispy and thinning, and I had no idea how old she was; I didn't care. Although, she was not so old that they had sent her to pasture, so to speak. I listened to her when I had to.

"She's dead, and she might have an illness that will make you all sick, so back the fuck up!" she ordered again in her brusque tone. Seffie—the closest friend I had—and I backed away from the gaunt figure.

"Yes, ma'am," we both muttered.

Seffie's hair was blond and straight, whereas mine was dark

and a constant frizz of curls. She was more beautiful than me too. Deborah said her hips were perfect for child-bearing, her breasts perfect for feeding.

I never got compliments from our teacher. Instead, whenever she looked at me, she clicked her teeth and muttered, "Baby won't even be able to latch on to feed; and you'll probably die in childbirth because your hips are so narrow."

Whenever she spoke like that, I felt shame to the core of my being because the other women would smirk and hold up their tits in my direction. All except Seffie. She would console me and say, "Don't listen to her. All types of women can be mothers." I would nod weakly.

When I tried to speak to the dead woman, before she died—she had a wild look in her eyes. But I could also see knowledge there. She reminded me of a very distant memory of my mother. They had had a similar demeanor—strength.

"Where do you come from?" I had asked her.

"I was with the free ones," she told me.

"Who are those?" I asked.

But she stopped speaking to me after that. She had just muttered, "There is no hope."

I never saw her take a single sip of water or bite to eat. She only sat in the corner of the corral and clutched her knees to her chest. After three days, just before she died, she screamed in agony and tried to stretch out her legs. The screaming lasted for what felt like eons. Eventually, she lay down and went to sleep. Then she died.

I turned to Seffie. "What do you think the free ones are?"

Seffie shrugged and pointed toward Deborah, who had ushered all the other women to the far corner of the corral. We joined them.

As I sat on the floor, I adjusted my white top, which just covered my breasts, and then smoothed my short linen skirt, which barely covered the area where my legs met. We called that area our rose. We all sat with our legs to the side—Deborah called it the mermaid pose. When I asked, she wouldn't explain a mermaid to me. I don't think she even knows.

The uniform was the only clothing I had ever known. It was all any of us had ever known.

"Gather around now, children," Deborah said, her tone cajoling. "We must wait for the Reaper-bot to come and take the dead one away."

I always hated it when Deborah called us children. I had been alive for sixty seasons. While in the corrals, we gauged our age by seasons, not years. Our lives only existed in seasons. Our seasons were a cycle of four distinct weather patterns. We could see them change through skylights in the ceiling. The slant of the ceiling meant I could see outside a mountain covered with trees. It was out there that I kept my heart. Where I hid my deepest feelings. It was in those trees I longed to rest my legs. My gaze lingered as I stared outside.

It got dark early during the winter season, and sometimes even a white blanket of snow covered everything. Once the white blanket disappeared, everything was left bare until the trees on the side of the mountain turned a beautiful green. Spring was my favorite season. Then came the hot summer season. Even though our corral had a cooling system, it still got hot and humid, making even breathing difficult. Just before it got to the cold, dark winter again, the leaves on the trees turned into a beautiful kaleidoscope of red, yellow, and orange.

"What is our purpose?" Deborah asked us.

She constantly interrupted me when I was looking at the

trees. All she wanted to do was keep us focused on our task. Our mission. To serve the Overseers.

We recited it to her.

We are the women.
We stay healthy,
Breed younglings,
And go peacefully,
When our work is done.
When the bullaman comes,
We willingly accept his gift,
And bear his seed.
And go peacefully,
When our work is done.

I wasn't sure where we were supposed to go peacefully to. But whenever the Reaper-bots took women out or brought different women in, all of them moved in a passive and compliant manner.

When the door to our corral opened, it hissed like a serpent. It startled most of the women, even Deborah; but I turned to look at the sound with awareness and not fear. It was the Reaper-bot. The droid was twice as tall as us and it seemed to walk funny, on legs that bent the wrong way. But it would be foolish to think it wasn't fast.

It stood on two metallic legs, with a body that hissed with a sound like breathing as it moved. The head looked like a silver-skinned human face, with two antennae where the eyebrows should have been.

Ignoring us, it went straight to the dead woman and picked her up.

Deborah always said that my curiosity was a curse to her. Every time she tried to teach us, I asked questions, and she hated it.

The other women listened passively, accepting what our leader said as the gospel truth.

Unlike them, I liked to explore all the areas of our corral, which was small, so I had been to every corner many times. I had even found a secret.

I often imagined that I was on a grand adventure by myself, with no one else to trouble me or tell me what to do or think. I imagined that I was in the forest on the mountain, touching the trees and holding the colorful leaves. Seffie called me foolish and refused to dream with me.

Unconsciously, I stood up. Behind me, I heard Deborah hiss for me to sit down as I walked toward the Reaper-bot. They came into the corral so seldom; I wanted to get closer and see what they were like. I also wanted to glimpse outside the door of our corral. I imagined outside was a beautiful forest of trees. Maybe the droid would take the dead woman out of the corral and lay her under the tree boughs on a bed of colorful leaves.

As I approached, the Reaper-bot turned to face me. Its red eyes flickered. I hesitated; the look frightened me. There was no emotion evident in the machine, but I sensed that if I took one more step, something terrible would happen to me.

I felt a sharp pinch on my ear, and Deborah wrenched my head to look up at her face. She was angry. She yanked me back to the corner of the corral, where the rest of the women stood huddled in a group, fidgeting with their feet and hands.

Deborah loosened her grip on my ear and then pushed me to stand behind her.

The Reaper-bot, no longer feeling threatened, reached the door, which opened automatically. I couldn't see out of it as it left.

"What are they going to do with her?" I asked Deborah

without looking in her direction. She didn't respond, so I turned to face her. "Why won't you tell us? What will they do with the body?"

Deborah said sternly, "They'll burn it: turn it to ash!" She clamped her mouth shut, like she had said too much. Her gaze shifted to a red light that was always on, in the corner of the corral.

Stepping toward me, she leaned in close to my ear and whispered harshly, "You need to stop doing this. They will take you away. And you are scaring the other women."

I glanced at the other women around us and noticed the fear in their eyes. With the announcement that the Reaper-bot would burn the woman's body, they had started to shift from foot to foot, their fingers unconsciously tapping the sides of their thighs and their gazes darting in different directions.

"Okay," I said. But I didn't mean it.

Deborah was the third teacher I could remember. She would take opportunities throughout the day to teach us as our herd did everything together in our corral, which was about forty strides by forty strides in area. I tuned Deborah out as she talked. There were times we were expected to attend to lessons, but mostly we were allowed to entertain ourselves by eating, sleeping, or frolicking.

In the frolicking area were toys that Deborah had taught us to use. The toys were eclectic and provided different forms of stimulation. We were encouraged to try the toys out on our own rose and on each other's roses. Some women were more inclined than others and would bring themselves to climax multiple times in the day. Deborah explained that what we were feeling was purely a physical response and to not let any emotion to get involved.

Seffie and I would play with the toys together, and at times when she used it on me, I felt a connection between me and her. But like Deborah said, I tried to shove that feeling deep down; sometimes

I was successful.

From early on, when the toys were first introduced to us, we were encouraged to use them on each other. If we wanted to use one on another woman, we just did—consent was not encouraged. A few women began to use the toys as a means to show dominance. But as long as Seffie and I stuck together, we kept those predators at bay.

Night was the best time, and I liked to watch the sun set through the skylight window. It dropped just behind the mountain, and as it cast its final fingers of red and orange onto the trees, I felt a sense of peace.

When we slept, we looked like a pile of dead bodies. Our legs were intertwined with each other's feet, hands, and waists. Some of us rested our heads on another's stomach or breasts, to preserve body heat.

I was used to the sounds of the night because I had known them my whole life. There was a steady humming from outside the walls of the corral. There was a voice, too, and sometimes I listened to it. It was the secret I had found.

Stretching my legs, I disentangled myself and immediately felt colder away from the herd. I crawled because it was quieter that way.

In the wall, across the room from where we slept, near the frolicking area, was a small crack. I found it and I didn't think anyone else did. But it was special. I had heard a voice through it. Most nights, just after the lights dimmed, I made my way to the crack in the wall.

The voice was older, and she said she was a mother. She asked that I call her Mother, and so I did. There was no voice as lovely as hers.

"Mother?" I whispered. "Are you there tonight?"

Silence. I leaned my head against the wall and waited.

"Zee?"

I think the voice had the same kind of tone as mine, as if she had a perpetual sore throat.

"Yes, Mother, I'm here," I answered. I moved quickly to my knees and placed the side of my head closer to the wall.

"I'm glad to hear your voice. I have something important to tell you," Mother said.

"I'm listening." The sense of urgency in her voice reminded me of the time when she first explained the Insemination Cycle to me, four seasons ago. When Deborah taught that lesson, her description of the event was clinical and detached and only physical; Mother, however, spoke about how it made her feel.

"The bullaman was brought in to our corral today," Mother said. I knew what that meant.

"Were you inseminated?" I asked cautiously. I didn't want to be pregnant. In the back of my mind, I recollected being taken from my birth mother. And I didn't want to have my own child taken from me. Mother told me that we used to raise our own children and that there might still be some places that women continue to do so.

"Not yet," she replied. "I hope to escape this time."

"What chances do you have of that?" I hoped she could escape this time too. When she shared her emotions about the event, I tried to empathize with her pain, but all I could feel was terror.

"Not good. He always knows. They always know. If the bullaman doesn't do it, the Reaper-bots do it with a syringe."

I gulped. "Isn't that painful?" I pressed my legs together at the thought, as if I was stopping the bullaman or the syringe then and there.

"We are used to it now," Mother said.

"What happens if you don't get inseminated?"

"Those who aren't go peacefully to a different corral; we don't know where."

She was silent for a moment, and I feared she might have left. I didn't want to be left alone.

"Tell me more about *before*," I pleaded, breaking the moment of silence.

Most people had forgotten our history. Mother said her mother had taught her. Her mother had been a free one. A feeling like a hand squeezing my stomach overwhelmed me when I thought this was it; that all I was to do in my life was sleep, eat, and shit, bear children, and then die.

She was silent again for a moment. "Before is where we belong."

We had spoken about *before* many times, but she couldn't really explain it except with vague descriptions. It was a distant memory somehow locked in our human conscience, like muscle memory.

"But what was it like?" I asked her.

Mother started to sing softly.

I see green on the trees and red roses too
They bloom in the spring, just like you do.
And I dream the dream of a beautiful world.

The clouds float by in billows of white,
The sun sets low with reds so bright.

And I dream the dream of a beautiful world.

Fat rain, drops from the sky,
The sun breaks through, clouds going by.
Friends greeting friends, "Hey, how are you?"
Lovers embrace, "I love you."

Babies born, innocent and free;
Their lives lived long, healthily.
And I dream the dream of a beautiful world.

"It's beautiful."

"It was a song my mother sang."

"What is *love*?" I asked. It was such a foreign word. I couldn't remember anyone ever saying *I love you.*

"Love is a powerful feeling connecting two people together."

"Do you love me?"

"Yes, my daughter, I love you very much."

Her answer stirred my blood passionately, but the feeling was fleeting as I remembered what she had said about the bullaman being released into her corral.

There were only two kinds of males that I knew of in the corrals: the bullaman and the nucksa. I had never seen a nucksa, and I only knew they existed because Mother had told me she had given birth to many males. They each had stayed with her until their twelfth season. They had then been taken away, and most of them had turned into nucksa. Some of them became bullaman.

"You must be ready," Mother said suddenly. "They are going to start the Insemination Cycle with your corral tomorrow."

I felt a lump form in my throat. "How do you know?" I asked

her.

"It is time. I keep track. You are sixty seasons. And that is when the Reaper-bots start the Insemination Cycle. You must keep track now too."

"What happens?"

"They will release a bullaman into the corral. Do not be alone. You need to huddle together as a herd. If you can, get inside the circle, close to the center. It will be harder for the bullaman to get to you."

"But he will get to someone else?" I glanced back at the women sleeping soundly across the corral.

"Yes, Zee. In time, he gets to all of you."

"But then what happens?"

"He will hold you down, lift his loincloth, and you will see his erect bullaman. He will put it inside of you, in your rose. It will be violent and it will hurt. After some time, he will give an aggressive shove at his release, and wait before pulling out. At that point, the bullaman will have inseminated you."

"And that means I will have a child?"

"It doesn't always take. If it doesn't, he keeps trying."

"What happens if I don't get impregnated?"

"They take you away and put you with the nucksa."

"Why is that a bad thing?" I asked.

Mother whispered, "I don't know. But I always feel afraid whenever I think about them. Something terrible happens to them."

Goose bumps made the hairs on my arms stand straight up as she spoke. I felt it too. It was a feeling of dark foreboding.

Mother paused. "I am almost two hundred seasons," she replied after a moment. "Soon, I will peacefully go, too."

I felt sadness at this declaration. "I will miss you," I told her.

"I will miss you too," she answered. "Now, come; you must learn the song. I will sing it again. It is the only thing I have that has been passed down to me. Only you were curious enough to listen to the crack in the wall. You are special."

I closed my eyes and listened to her voice. By the fourth time, I started to sing along. And once she was finished and I returned to the herd, I kept singing the song in my head. One line stood out: *And I dream the dream, of a beautiful world.*

Chapter 2

ξ

The Bullaman

I awoke with a heavy feeling in the pit of my stomach. I felt like retching my guts out. Deborah stood over me, her mood also dark.

"Get the fuck up; you need to eat something," she said in her unpleasant way.

I watched her as she walked toward the trough. Our feeding area was located in the corral corner opposite the piss and shit drain. But frankly, the smell at both places was the same. Deborah must be at least twice my age, if not more. I heard her mention once that we were her fourth herd. She would stay with us until our first few inseminations and then she would be moved to another herd.

She seemed old, but she wasn't ugly. She was just bitchy.

Hanging over the trough was a shoot that dumped in a red porridge mixture; I didn't know what was in it, and it didn't taste like anything.

The other women at the trough moved aside as Deborah took her place. She squatted down, cupped some food with her hand, and brought it to her mouth. Watching her eat didn't moisten my mouth with saliva or calm my already anxious gut. I had no desire to eat. But I remembered the woman who had died. She hadn't eaten. I needed to stay healthy.

Dragging myself to my feet, I looked around and spied Seffie not far away. I walked toward her, my feet chilly against the laminate flooring.

"Seffie," I said.

She looked up and then gently moved one of the other women aside to make room for me. The shuffle spread down the entire length of the trough, until the woman at the end was pushed out of the way and could no longer eat.

She stood with a scowl on her face. Aside from Deborah, Deliav was the meanest woman in our corral. Most of us stayed away from her because she liked to fight and grab other women's roses aggressively. It was a pitiful attempt to show dominance.

"What the fuck?" she said, storming toward me as I sat next to Seffie. "Who pushed me?"

No one responded. But I looked in her direction, which was enough of an admission of guilt for her.

"Bitch!" she said as she charged me and grabbed me by the hair, yanking me from the trough.

Deborah barely looked up. Fighting between the women wasn't uncommon and she let us figure out our own politics.

"Let go!" I hollered. "I didn't fucking push you!"

She twisted her fingers in my hair, and I felt tears pouring down the sides of my cheeks. I reached up and grabbed her hair in return. She tried to jerk her head out of the way, but I had long arms and I was fast.

I clawed at the black strands of her hair and yanked back. Her neck bent, but she tried to fight it.

Releasing my hair, she wound up to punch me in the face, but as she tried to back up to give herself leverage, I yanked her head down to my knee, which made contact with her nose.

Deliav let out a cry that echoed off the walls of the corral.

I stepped back. Deliav fell to the floor, blood pouring from her nose, mixing with the tears from her eyes. I made a sudden move toward her and she flinched. That would help her remember I was not to be messed with.

Deliav backed away and I returned to the trough.

When I was done, I followed Seffie over to the piss and shit drain, and just as I finished relieving myself, the lights in the corral dimmed.

"What's going on?" Seffie asked.

"Shh, I think the bullaman is being released in our corral."

"How do you know?" There was a quiver of fear in her voice.

"Mother told me." Seffie gave me a sidelong look. She knew about the crack in the wall. But she was never inclined to come and listen with me.

I watched as Deborah had moved away from the rest of the herd, toward the center of the corral, where she stood facing the door. She motioned the other women to stay back and watch.

A moment later, the door opened with a loud hiss. I craned my neck to get a glimpse at what was happening. At first, I thought it was just a Reaper-bot. It entered the door and took position between the herd and the entrance.

We knew the Reaper-bots looked after us, but they didn't own us. The Overseers owned us and our farm.

The Overseer was twice as tall as me. Its chest looked human enough, very muscular, chiseled, and hard as stone. It had hands like ours, but larger and stronger. On one finger was a gold ring.

It did not wear a shirt. Instead several leather straps criss-crossed over its shoulders down to a loincloth.

The legs were similar to those of the Reaper-bot, in that they seemed to bend the wrong way, but coarse black hair covered them. Its feet were different also: round and hard hooves.

Two long horns came out of its head. Its nose protruded from its body and at the tip was its mouth. A metal ring was pierced through its nose.

A second Overseer entered the corral, and it looked as foreboding as the first. In its hand, it held a leash, and attached to the leash was the bullaman.

As I looked at him, a feeling of nausea turned my stomach and I burped a foul-tasting stench into my throat. The bullaman was younger than Deborah but older than us. There was a tinge of red in his very long black beard. His black hair was also long, and it was straggly and unkempt. His body looked leathery and strong. Not like the Overseers' bodies, but muscular and healthy nonetheless. Deborah said that the Overseers took good care of the bullamans, making sure they didn't get sick because so few males were allowed to become them. He may have seemed handsome if not for the repulsion I felt as I looked at him.

The Overseer yanked on the leash, saying something in grunts, snorts, and snuffs, and the bullaman stepped forward. The Overseer reached up to unclip the leash and then stepped back.

Not bothering to look at his captors, the bullaman entered the corral and headed straight toward Deborah, who was waiting for him.

When he reached her, she lowered herself to the ground, lay on her back, and lifted her skirt, exposing her rose to the bullaman.

I watched the bullaman's face change right before my eyes. He wanted Deborah. I could tell because his vision examined her rose like he wanted to devour her.

He got down on his knees and sniffed her in the private area. His hands lifted her bra above her breasts, and she let him.

I shifted my gaze to Deborah. Her face was placid and vacant.

His fingers pinched and squeezed her breasts, and I saw her take a sharp breath in. For some reason, that invigorated the bullaman; from his loincloth, I could see his bullaman became erect. It was as long as a hand and hard.

He took the erection in his hands and guided it toward Deborah's rose. When it touched her, he gave a shove, and his erection disappeared inside of her. Once again, Deborah took in a sharp breath as the bullaman slid himself in and out of her.

After only a couple of minutes, the bullaman's face began to tighten. His breath became heavier, and his muscles started to clench and bulge. Suddenly, he moaned loudly and pushed hard inside one more time. He waited for a few seconds before pulling out his bullaman. I saw it had gone flaccid.

Deborah pulled her skirt and bra back down to cover herself, then she stood and walked toward the herd. They were still standing by the trough, opposite of the piss and shit drain, where Seffie and I stood.

The Overseers seemed content with what they had seen; they exited. And we were alone with the bullaman.

He was still kneeling on the floor in the center of the corral.

Seffie and I made our way back to the herd, giving him a very wide berth. The other women were fidgeting and dancing on tiptoes.

Deborah was speaking. "Remember what I have taught you. It is easy to be inseminated," she said. "When the bullaman takes you the first time, you will feel a small bit of pain, but it will go away. Some of you might even experience some pleasure. A good feeling will wash over your whole body."

"Will all of us?" a voice asked.

"No, only some," Deborah answered. "But if you let yourself be taken by him, you have a better chance of feeling pleasure. If you fight him, it will be more painful."

"How should we do it?" Deliav asked. Her face had dried blood on her chin from my knee colliding with her nose.

"It is best to offer yourself to him, just as I did. You will feel hesitant at first. But it is easier just to offer yourself. Once he starts hunting the ones who have stayed away, he gets more aggressive."

"Are all bullaman the same?" I asked. It wasn't curiosity so much as the fear they were.

Deborah turned to me. "No. The young ones who are inseminating for the first time are just as unsure and hesitant as the heifers." Her face turned darker. "But soon enough, you see their hunger." She was quiet for a moment. "It is always better to offer yourself, especially to this bullaman. He likes the thrill of a chase, and when he catches you, he takes you forcefully."

"You know him?"

"He and I have done this many times. There are only a handful of bullaman on the farm. He is one of the best; he inseminates more women than all the others. That is why they let him be more aggressive with the hesitant women."

Turning around, I once again looked at the bullaman. He had recovered and was watching us at the herd intently. Our eyes made contact. His were so dark, yet I saw a flicker of desire come over him and I backed away, trying to put a few women between him and me.

"What the fuck?" I whispered at Seffie. She clutched my arm as we watched Deliav move closer to the bullaman and then coyly backed away until she reached his side and knelt down.

Hesitantly, she reached toward his bullaman and began to caress it. It grew hard again, and the bullaman grabbed her by the shoulders, lowering her to her back. She parted her legs and lifted her skirt, exposing her rose.

It was as quick as before, but after he released inside of her, she lowered herself to his lap and rested her head there. The bullaman accepted her submission and brushed her hair softly.

Deborah whispered to the rest of us. "Deliav is a good woman; you all could learn a lot from her."

I wanted to smack the lips off her mouth.

Chapter 3

ξ

The Insemination

At the start, the women in my herd were hesitant and unsure. A few would offer themselves each day, which seemed to satiate the bullaman's appetite.

However, as the number of women inseminated grew around him, I saw the dynamics of our herd changing. The number of hesitant dwindled.

Deborah spent her days with us, the hesitant. She constantly encouraged us to offer our bodies to the bullaman. But at nighttime, she returned to the bullaman's side, like a second-in-command.

As my herd's numbers dwindled around me, I noticed the bullaman watched us, the hesitant, more intently. We offered a challenge to his desires.

"It will be worse later," Deborah said to Seffie and me. "Better to just get it over with."

On the fifth day after the bullaman joined our corral, I awoke and found that only two women remained with me, the rest had offered themselves to the bullaman. There was Carralin, a shy, passive woman I didn't know very well.

Seffie stayed with me, but her resolve was weakening.

"Zee, I think I am going to do it," she said to me finally. My heart suddenly felt hollow and I looked at my friend. I could see the fear on her face. She was torn between her loyalty to me and adherence to the herd. But even more than that, she appeared torn between following the order of things or supporting me, her friend. Deborah arrived and looked at her with an approving expression.

"You can't," I replied quietly. "I need you." I wanted to tell her it was her decision to make, but I couldn't, because something about all of it felt so wrong.

"Okay," she said. "But only because I am your friend. But you have to know that I don't want to be taken forcefully. If Carralin goes, I will go next. And then you will be alone."

"I don't understand," I lied to her. I also felt the overwhelming pull to obey. I felt the pull of the herd. I didn't like being different from my peers.

"Understand what?" Deborah overheard and answered for my friend.

I turned to her. This woman was supposed to be our teacher. But the more I watched, the more I felt that she was put here to make us obedient. She was angry with those who questioned, and benevolent to those who didn't. "I don't want this to happen. Why would I offer myself to him when I don't want this to happen? I will fight him taking me, even if it kills me!"

Deborah was unsympathetic. "It is the way of things. If you do manage to fight off the bullaman, then the Reaper-bot will come and take you away."

"That's better than letting that piece of filth touch any part of me!" Spittle flew out of my mouth as I spoke. "I should be able to give consent or not!"

Deborah shook her head and turned her attention to Carralin. The short, red-haired woman was on the brink of tears as Deborah took her by the hand and slowly escorted her toward the center of the corral.

Seffie gave me a stern look.

"Come to the piss and shit drain with me," I said to her.

She nodded sadly.

I was used to being inconspicuous when I pissed, but everyone was watching me this time, even the bullaman. As I released, I saw him stand up.

Finishing quickly, I pulled my skirt, which had been up around my belly, down to cover my rose, and stood next to Seffie.

The bullaman's face shifted into a mischievous smile like he knew a great secret he was about to share with us. His hands clenched and unclenched, and he licked his lips as he took his first step toward us. He completely ignored Carralin, who Deborah had deposited at his feet.

Look at her! I wanted to scream. *Take her instead!* I cried guiltily.

But he tilted his head down, looking at us through the tops of his eyes. His bushy eyebrows were dark and foreboding.

"Come," I hissed at Seffie. "Walk quickly, but don't run. We must get to the far corner. If he takes us, I don't want it to be here." I felt her body, as it touched mine, resist slightly.

"Zee?" Her voice was hesitant.

The bullaman was walking toward us, and I tried to steer Seffie in a different direction to keep others between us and the man.

But he continued to approach us in a steady gait.

"Now! Run!" I yelled at Seffie. I screamed at the bullaman, "Fuck off!" and took off, assuming Seffie was right on my heels.

But it was like she hadn't heard me. She froze in place. The bullaman took only a moment to reach her. "Leave her alone!" I yelled, waving my arms. But he ignored me now. I wanted to run up and punch him, or tackle him, but I was afraid he would turn on me.

Guiltily, I watched as Seffie stared at the bullaman.

I noticed his bullaman was erect, and it was pointing out from his body from under his loincloth. He stopped in front of Seffie and grabbed her breasts, the same way he had all the others. But this time there was no caressing; it was harsh and violent. He squeezed her nipples between his fingers until Seffie let out a cry of pain. But her fear kept her immobile, and she almost collapsed except that the bullaman wrapped his arm around her back and held her up.

Her cries caused the bullaman's eyes to go wild in lust. His mouth opened slightly, and he breathed heavily through his nostrils. Violently, he threw her down, and the back of her head hit the floor.

He was already lifting his loincloth, and I saw his bullaman again; it was engorged, pulsating and quivering. With his knees, he kept Seffie's legs apart so he could guide his bullaman into her rose. With an aggressive shove, it disappeared inside of her.

I couldn't take my eyes off Seffie's face. She seemed so small, so powerless, so broken, lying there. As the bullaman inserted himself into her, I saw tears form in the corners of her eyes, her mouth stuck in a silent scream. Each thrust of the bullaman's erection made her look like she was going to be sick. Finally, the bullaman gave two last thrusts, waited, and then pulled himself out and stood up, leaving her prone body on the floor. He stalked back to the herd in the center of the corral. His lips were smacking together, his hand rubbing his bullaman.

I ran to Seffie. "I'm sorry. I'm so sorry," I said to her over and over as I knelt beside her. There was a tiny bit of blood between her legs, making her rose glisten redder. She quickly covered herself with her skirt, and I helped her to her feet.

"Don't let him do it to you," she whispered hoarsely. She turned and took a step toward the center of the corral to join the others. I needed to stop her. But I didn't know what to say or do.

"What do you feel?" I asked her, catching her arm. It wasn't just curiosity; it was fear. I wanted to fight. But could I?

She didn't answer right away. "I feel ashamed," she said sadly.

I thought I understood what she meant. He had taken her without her permission.

"But was it painful?"

"Yes. But it hurts more here." She pointed to her chest.

"When he grabbed your breasts?" I asked naively.

She negated my question with a shake of her head. "No. I feel empty, ravaged, in my chest. And it feels like he is still inside me."

I released her arm, and she walked the rest of the way to the herd, now clearly one of them. Her gaze stayed on me, and I met her eyes with a sad stare.

The lights dimmed. The signal night had descended. The other women huddled together near the bullaman now. The dynamics of the herd had shifted from Deborah as the leader, to the bullaman. Carralin also offered herself to the bullaman at the urging of the others.

I curled up as best I could. I shivered from the cold floor, missing the heat of my herd. I briefly wondered if I could sneak into the herd, to be with them, and refrain capture by the bullaman.

I kept my gaze fixed on the bullaman. He was sitting cross-legged on the floor, with the other women curled around him. But he watched me. As it got darker, all I could see were the dark lights of his eyes reflecting the night.

Finally, he lay down and closed his eyes. I waited a few more minutes. Silently, I crawled to the edge of the herd, but the women moved away from me slightly.

I tried my best to stay awake, but my blinks got longer until I finally allowed myself to fall asleep.

As I fell asleep, I dreamed of Seffie's insemination; even in my dream, I gagged in fear of the bullaman. But I also felt shame. I felt guilty for leaving her. I should have done something.

A warm touch on my back awakened me. It was still dimly lit, and I glanced at the herd in the middle of the corral; I could make out the women's sleeping shapes.

A hand slid around my waist and grasped my breast, and I instantly knew who was behind me. A wildness took over my mind and will. It was pure luck that as I jabbed my elbow backward as quickly as I could, it smashed the bullaman in the nose. It was a hard blow, and I felt sharp pins and needles run up my forearm. He bellowed like an angry bull, and I jumped to my feet as his hands clutched his face.

He also stood up. Slower. Intentionally.

I stayed in a crouched position, ready to bolt.

Tears streamed down his cheeks, mixing with the blood from his nose.

"You shouldn't have done that! Bitch!" he swore at me. His voice was deep and low.

His shout woke the other women, and I could hear them murmuring. I could even feel them watching me in the darkness. The faint early morning light from the skylight enabled me to make out his form.

I backed away in my crouched position, keeping my vision fixed on him.

"I won't give myself to you," I said to him.

He laughed. "Heifers are all the same. Even ones like you." He brushed aside the blood and tears. A loud snort cleared his nostrils. He licked his lips and charged at me, but I dodged him easily. He was big, but he was slower than me. I could smell the stench of his body odor as it lingered behind him like a cape, a trail that marked his passing.

His fingers clenched as he turned and snorted aggressively.

I gulped visibly—so much anger, so much dominance! And the decision was entrenched in my mind. He would have to kill me because I would fight to my death to keep him from me.

This time, he was prepared for my movement. He held out his arm as he charged, and his fist hit me in the chest, sending me flying to the ground. I gasped, the air was knocked out of my lungs, and I struggled to get to my feet.

But he was on me quickly. His hands were strong, and he easily held down my shoulders. Then he reached down with the other hand for his loincloth.

I thrashed my arms, trying to move them. But they were locked to my sides at the elbows, each hit little more than a nuisance to the bullaman. He was salivating, breathing rapidly and heavily.

As I looked into his eyes, I saw his disgusting hunger there. I could tell he loved my squirming and fighting. It was something I couldn't comprehend. So, I suddenly lay still.

This caught him off guard. He expected my struggle. Even though my legs were still clenched together, he pulled his bullaman out of his loincloth and lowered it toward my rose. He was straddling my legs, so I was not sure how he would force himself inside me. He licked his hand and wetted his bullaman with his spit.

In answer to my thought, he slid his hand between my thighs and there was nothing I could do to stop it, despite my clenching them together.

The sickening smile on his face was so arrogant; he relaxed for the briefest of moments. I rammed my knee up into the base of his bullaman.

The expression on his face changed from one of pleasure to one of intense agony, and he rolled off me, clutching his stomach. I stood up, and with my bare foot, I kicked him in the bullaman over and over again until he pleaded with me to stop. With one more solid kick to his groin, I stopped.

I must have nicked an artery or vein with a toenail because suddenly he reached down with his hand and clutched his bullaman. Blood poured through his fingers, and there was horror on his face. The women from the herd scattered and fidgeted nervously, glancing from me to Deborah, to the bullaman.

I had never seen so much blood before, and it was pooling at his feet.

Exhausted, I fell to the floor, unable to exert any more energy. The bullaman stayed prone and in a fetal position, unmoving except for his chest, which heaved like a swelling ocean.

Suddenly the lights came on, and the door to the corral opened.

The two alien Overseers from earlier entered the room. The Reaper-bot followed them. The droid dragged a hose behind it. It went to the bullaman and sprayed the blood off the floor and toward the piss drain. As it worked, the sun's light peeked through the window, brightening the corral.

The Overseers spoke to each other in tones and words that sounded only like grunts and snorts. They turned their gaze onto me, and fear crept into my heart as it raced faster.

After all the blood was washed away, the Reaper-bot picked up the bullaman and carried him out of the corral. One of the

Overseers took a leash from its belt and wrapped it around my neck, where it clicked in place. With a violent pull, the Overseer yanked me to my feet. I stumbled forward.

"Where are they taking me?" I yelled. "What is going to happen?"

"This is of your own making," Deborah shouted at me coldly. In some act of excommunication, she turned her back on me and made the other women do the same.

"Seffie, please tell Mother, through the crack. Please!" I begged her. And the Overseer pulled me through the door before I could hear Seffie's reply.

Chapter 4

ξ

The White Domes

The bullaman's whole frame was defeated and slouched. His face had gone deathly pale. I could still see a trail of blood dripping down his inner thigh. Good, I must have kicked him harder than I thought I did.

The Overseers led us into a new place, a dramatic contrast from the corral I had been in. As soon as I stepped over the threshold, I entered a white, sterile environment. The floors were tile, polished and glassy. The walls were also of the same material, but not tiles. The Overseers kept me far away from the bleeding bullaman. Next to the door was a television screen, and I immediately connected the fact that it showed the inside of the corral from the angle of the red light in the upper corner of the room. I could see Seffie standing halfway from the herd, facing the door I had just exited.

The Overseer holding my leash motioned at the bullaman and spoke to the other Overseer. Once again, their language sounded like snorts and grunts. I couldn't even begin to form the sounds that made up their language.

The other one snuffed.

He responded. The other turned to lead the Reaper-bot and bullaman down the hall.

As the Overseer leading me turned down the very long hall, I looked at the screens next to the doors. We passed at least twenty corrals, and inside each of them, I could see more humans like me. Some were all women; some were not women—I knew instantly they were the nucksa—and some corrals were made up of both.

"Where are you taking me?" I asked the Overseer.

He ignored my pleas, and his face winced each time I spoke, like my words were just primitive sounds and animal-like.

However, my question was soon answered as we approached the end of the hall. A massive airlock door opened with a swish and hiss, and suddenly a brilliant natural light shone through. The sun.

The skylight in the corral ceiling had allowed us to see the sky, which helped us tell the different seasons. But I had never felt the heat of the sun. Mother had felt it once.

As I stepped outside, I realized that my corral and the others that I had passed by were part of a giant white dome. I could see countless other domes. Mine was situated on a hill overlooking the rest. Humans moved in transit between domes; some were loaded on waiting transports that hovered above the ground.

As the Overseer led me away from the corral, he turned a corner, and behind me stood a massive building. It was white, like everything else. I watched as a group of nucksa followed a woman in a singular line. She was encouraging the nucksa to follow her into the white building. In my heart, I had an ominous sense they shouldn't follow her, but they did.

A voice startled me, and I turned, as did the Overseer. This Overseer who spoke was smaller than the one with my leash. It wore the same kind of fabric all the Overseers wore, but it was more colorful and covered more skin on its body. It seemed like a she.

The older one holding my leash grunted.

The younger Overseer's face dropped.

Glancing from me to the younger Overseer, the one holding

my leash contemplated something, then held out my leash to the younger one.

It took the leash, and I followed it meekly.

The younger Overseer talked to me nonstop in rapid snorts and grunts as it brought me to a golden chariot. Nothing was pulling the chariot; it hovered about a foot off the ground. We got inside.

Reaching down, the Overseer touched her golden ring to a blue light, and the chariot moved. Somehow, I thought, the ring must connect their consciousness to different tools—like to drive this chariot. I was very proud of myself for thinking of such a thing.

We whizzed by the domes. I thought there must be thousands upon thousands of humans kept in the corrals. But to what purpose?

We came to a stop in front of another white-domed building. This one was different; it was smaller, with multiple domes all connected. The young Overseer stepped off the chariot and led me through an airlock door that opened as she approached.

Inside, I realized that this was her corral. It was superior to mine. She had furniture suited to her form. The floors were glassy white marble tile, and the walls were white glass as well.

We passed a room, and I caught a glimpse of another human. He had to be hundreds of seasons or more—his hair was gray and his skin wrinkly. He saw me too, but he didn't get up to follow. He was sitting cross-legged on a chair, just watching the house.

The Overseer snorted. She opened a door, and we entered a room of clear glass. She placed me into a cylindrical room and closed me in it. A moment later, water blasted me from all sides. I tried to scream, but the liquid kept hitting me in the face and mouth. Dirt fell off my body, and my wild hair flew behind me as I moved my head to escape the water.

"Please stop!" I begged, but the Overseer watched for a few

moments longer before turning it off. They had made us take showers in the corral, but there, they only used a hose to spray us, and we would wash.

With the water shut off, the Overseer pulled me out by the leash, and I stood in front of it as it took off my rags and tossed them into a cubby on the wall. She took out a white smock and put it on me, talking unintelligibly the entire time.

Hours passed before I felt sleepy. My Overseer had spent that time brushing and cutting my hair. When she was finished, it was late, and the Overseer who took me out of the corral entered the room and spoke.

The younger one attached my leash to a post beside her bed, pointed at a cushion by her feet, and spoke. I was supposed to sleep there, I concluded.

Once the light was turned out, it was dark, but I couldn't sleep; I missed my herd. Seffie had always helped keep me warm. Her breathing had helped me feel safe and secure. But the Overseer's loud exhales were disturbing. Cautiously, I raised my hand to the collar around my neck. It was a rudimentary device, and it took me only a few moments to work out how it was connected. A small indent on the back was all it took. I pressed it and it unclipped. The Overseer was fast asleep in its bed. Placing it back around my throat, I knew now wasn't the time to escape.

My eyes became more accustomed to the darkness and objects began to take shape. The room was circular, and there were various pictures on the wall, along with a screen, like the ones I had seen in the white domes. The Overseer lay on a white structure, and it looked soft. Raising my hand, I ran it along the fabric that covered her. Her small horns were pressed into a pillow, and one of her hoofed feet stuck out from under the blanket.

Remembering the other human, I stealthily walked toward the door. It opened with a hiss at my approach, and I stopped and looked back at the Overseer. She remained asleep. Cautiously, I exited the room. The house was quiet. I recognized the door that led to the place where I had been washed, and I moved away from it. I was more concerned with finding the other human.

The home's main living area was extensive, and I saw furniture I couldn't sit on because my legs didn't work the same way as the Overseers. The chair was a zigzagged shape that allowed the Overseers' legs to fold up under them. I would just slide off if I tried to sit on it.

The older human was gone, and I wondered where he could be. Leaving to search, I found an immaculate white room with a table, counters, and odd-looking bubbles with doors. They sat on the floor like chests or pantries. I approached one of the bubbles and grasped its silver handle. When I pulled, there was a hissing sound, and a door opened into a smaller cupboard. Cold air rushed at me, and I shivered. On the shelves, I saw pieces of meat wrapped in clear cellophane. I sniffed, but I could not smell anything and closed the door.

A sound startled me—behind me was the older human.

"What are you doing?" he asked me. His tone was neither friendly nor mean; it was just indifferent. I got a better look at him. He was about the same height as me. His hair was gray, and he had brown spots on his face and arms. The skin around his eyes, cheeks, and mouth was wrinkly. He wore a white smock, similar to mine. It was so foreign; I had never seen someone older than Deborah before.

"I was looking for you," I replied.

His face twisted oddly. “Well, I hope you never find me in there.” He motioned to the bubble I had just opened. “That’s the fridge.”

“Fridge?” I asked.

“It’s where they keep their food.”

“Oh, right,” I replied. “What is your name?”

He turned and walked away. “You shouldn’t be out. If Ki’ichpanil finds you, you might be punished.”

“You don’t have a leash,” I said, following him.

“I’ve been in this family for a long time. I have earned some freedom. You have not, and you have no idea how lucky you are.”

“What do you mean?”

“I assume you were in the corrals?”

“Yes.”

“Then you are lucky the daughter wanted you as a pet.”

“A pet?”

“A pet, and you will understand all that that includes as time goes on. But it does mean you will get to live a long life, unlike those who are left in the corrals.”

He walked out of the room, and I followed him. “Wait, what do you know?”

“I know the family cares for me. Now, you should go back to the bedroom. Tomorrow Ki’ichpanil will start training you.”

“Who is Ki’ichpanil?” I asked.

“She is your *Overseer*. Your owner.”

“How do you know her name?”

He turned to leave again.

“Wait, what is your name?” I said again.

He sniffed. “My name doesn’t matter. I’m not here to be friends with you.”

"My name is Zee," I continued, unabated.

A slight growl came from his throat, and he sneered as he turned to look at me. "Fine. My name is Barru. The name my Overseers gave me is *Esclavista*."

I was shocked. "You can speak their language?"

"No, I can say a few words, but I cannot speak it. The human vocal cords cannot make the sounds required to speak their language. If they heard me, it would sound like a poorly muffled imitation. But I understand everything they say."

"I wish I could understand them."

"You will, over time. Now, get back to your owner. There is only one rule in the house: don't make *Bejlae'* mad."

"What?"

"The Overseer who owns you is Ki'ichpanil; her father's name is *Bejlae'*. He is a butcher and doesn't care about us one way or the other. Ki'ichpanil is much nicer. You will find in time that they have complex personalities. Some are cruel. Some are kind. Now go, please, before they wake up."

Barru returned to the furniture I had first seen him on. He curled into a fetal position and closed his eyes. He clearly would not speak with me anymore.

I returned to Ki'ichpanil's bedroom. I was glad I knew her name, and that she was a female. When the door hissed open, she stirred slightly but didn't wake up.

I returned to the pillow on the floor. I tried to curl up in a fetal position as Barru had, but I just couldn't feel comfortable. I was too used to my herd keeping me warm and snug. I wondered, briefly, what Barru meant when he said I was lucky because I would get to live a long life, unlike those in the corrals. I knew Mother was about two hundred seasons. How many seasons was Barru?

Chapter 5

ξ

The Slaughter House

At the back of the alien's home was another room. Ki'ichpanil introduced me to it to start my training. The room was also a dome and bolted into the wall were specially carved handholds. I realized quickly that I could climb using the holds, all the way to the pinnacle of the ceiling and back down again.

It didn't occur to me why this room existed. But it was made for humans. The Overseers' hoof feet prevented them from climbing, like I did.

At first, Ki'ichpanil let me roam and move freely. But eventually, using the power of her ring, she would force me to move in certain ways. I would climb certain paths, and if I strayed, she would send agonizing pain to my head. The pain would only subside when I went the way she wanted me to. I quickly learned to anticipate moves cautiously, so that at the slightest inkling of pain, I would correct my path.

There was other equipment for me to use, such as a machine with a tread, which when I stepped on it, started to turn and I could run. This was my favorite. I could run for hours.

Of course, Ki'ichpanil taught me other things too. She would say commands, and I needed to learn the word and obey. The first command was to *come* to her, and it took me awhile to understand the intonation of the sound that came out of her mouth. As Barru had said, I couldn't speak the language, but I was beginning to understand it.

She also taught me to stay in one place, like a good pet. Anytime that I didn't obey the command, she would send pain to my head.

I didn't spend every minute with Ki'ichpanil. Her and Bejlae' would disappear sometimes, but I had freedom to enter the training room. I would climb, run, roll toys like balls around. And every day, I could feel my strength growing. My endurance improved immensely.

One morning, I woke up with Ki'ichpanil, and immediately I could tell it was a different kind of day. She dressed differently and didn't speak to me.

I followed her out of the room. When we arrived in the kitchen, Barru was already there, getting his food. I walked up to him. "What is going on? Something is different."

He nodded. "Ki'ichpanil will go to school today."

"School?"

"It is a training for her. But she must travel to the far side of the white-domed farm, to the town."

"Town?" This word was so confusing to me.

"Most of the Overseers live and work there. The others live in their massive cities, far from here."

"Oh," I reply.

Ki'ichpanil was anxious as she placed my food in front of me. I could tell from her tone as she spoke to Bejlae'.

"The upside," Barru says, "is that you will have much more freedom during the days. Bejlae' doesn't care what we do."

"Okay." I kept eating. I hadn't seen Seffie for so long, and I was curious if I could find her and talk to her, maybe find Mother too.

When the house was silent and Barru had curled up on his furniture again, I tentatively approached the door that led outside. I knew it was motion-activated, but I wondered if I would be able to enter again. The thought fled as there was a whoosh of air, and I could see outside. A burst of cold air hit me, and I saw snow on the ground. I knew what it was, because back in the corrals, we used the sight of it to tell the seasons.

It was frigid on my bare feet. But I persevered and exited into the outdoors. There was a lot of activity, more than I remembered before. Many aliens were working on various things; some were riding the golden chariots while others led humans in groups of twenty or thirty. Some were working on the buildings.

When Ki'ichpanil first brought me home, she had used the golden chariot. The walk was much longer. Most Overseers didn't give me the slightest attention, since my leash and collar signified that I was a pet. I noticed a few other humans who also had collars and leashes. I didn't stop to speak with them because I needed to find Seffie and Mother first.

The white dome that had been my home appeared in front of me, and I sped up; a feeling of warmth came over my body. Suddenly, I stopped. Bejlae' exited the white-domed building. He didn't notice me, but I felt I shouldn't let him see me. He kept walking, and when I thought it was safe to continue, I entered the building.

I ran to the door that had been my corral. When I looked into the screen beside the door, I could see my herd, but I couldn't see Seffie right away. There was a new bullaman; he was lounging in the center of the corral. Deborah and all the women huddled around him. Most of them had rounded bellies. This bullaman was younger, probably only a few seasons older than me.

Then I noticed Seffie; she looked to be almost a couple

seasons pregnant. I remembered what Mother had told me long ago: that women would be pregnant for three seasons and give birth in the fourth. The youngling would remain with its Mother for twelve seasons, then be taken away.

I pulled myself away from the screen, went one corral down, and looked into the screen showing Mother's corral. I could see an Overseer inside, prodding all the women into two different lines. In one line were the pregnant women with rounded bellies; in the other line, women who weren't pregnant.

At the front of each line was a pet.

The Overseer went to the corral door, and I looked for a place to hide. I couldn't see any options, so I walked farther down the hall, away from the exit. I squatted down when I heard the airlock open.

The human-pet leading the women exited first, and the unpregnant ones followed her. The Overseer came out with them, about halfway down the line. One of the women at the back seemed familiar to me; was that Mother? I had never seen Mother, but there was a deep sense in my being it was her.

Getting to my feet, I hurried to catch up to them.

"Mother?" I whispered at the end of the line. A few women's heads turned in my direction.

"Zee?" a woman three from the end said.

"Mother!"

I walked up beside her.

"Why are you here?" Her gaze rested on my collar and leash.

"Where are they taking you?" I asked her.

"I don't know, Daughter," she whispered. "But I am happy I got to see you, even if it was incredibly foolish on your part."

"I'm sorry, but I wanted to see you. And Seffie."

"Hush now. I want you not to follow any longer. Go back,

Daughter."

When I looked at the other women, I could see anxiousness in their eyes. Most of them followed meekly, but I could see fingers twitching, throats gulping, and I knew they were afraid.

"But I want to stay with you." I whispered because I was worried the murmuring from the other women would cause the Overseer to turn around.

Mother shook her head softly. "Remember the song. Pass it on to your own daughter."

I stopped walking and watched them exit the building. As if some force compelled me, I decided to follow. But I stayed at a reasonable distance behind them. When they exited the white-domed building, they turned and followed the road leading up to the white factory. The pet at the front walked calmly and confidently.

There were a dozen corrals set up; a couple of them were filled with herds. The two I saw were nucksa. Mother's herd was ushered into the third corral, and they huddled together to keep warm. The human-pet leading them stayed with them.

Each of the corrals had its own pet. The nucksa herds had women as pets.

I watched with fascination as an Overseer came to the first corral and commanded the pet to bring the herd it was leading inside.

"Here."

The herd followed the pet in meekly and obediently. Each of the nucksa had to be only the same age as me. But they looked plumper than me, like they had been well fed.

When it was Mother's herd's time to enter, I wanted to follow, but there were so many Overseers around, it was difficult to keep close. So I joined at the end of the line. I didn't want Mother to see me because she wouldn't be pleased to know I had followed.

The factory was large, and a terrible smell hit my nostrils as soon as we entered. The woman in the herd got antsier. The pet leading them turned around and said: "It's okay; you will be safe in a moment. Just through that door up there."

Her voice was reassuring and calm, and I wanted to trust her. But there was something wrong. I could feel it palpably.

The hall we walked through was narrow, and we had to go single file. I kept my eyes firmly affixed on the pet at the lead as we approached a metal door. This hall was white marble like all the rest of the buildings.

As the pet arrived at the door, she diverted to the left, where an Overseer stood watching the humans. Immediately a gate closed behind her, forcing the herd through the door. As I got closer, I could see into the room. It looked a lot like the shower room Ki'ichpanil had taken me into.

The women huddled together nervously.

When it was my turn to enter the room, the Overseer stopped me.

He snorted, and part way through his phrase, I understood what the words were: "*...you doing here*?" He opened the gate and pulled me aside. His gold ring ran over my barcode, and a holographic screen appeared above his hand.

My eyes lighted at the sound of Ki'ichpanil's name.

"*You...come...*" he snorted.

I glanced back longingly as the metal door closed on the room that Mother had entered.

The Overseer opened another door, and the other pet and I entered another immaculate, white-tiled room. He led us to a mat on the floor, and I sat down with the pet.

"Why do you lead the herds?"

"For this," she replied as the Overseer returned with a bowl of food.

"What happens to the others?"

"They go to the *Carnicero*."

"What is that?"

"You don't know what this is, do you?"

"No," I replied.

"This is a slaughterhouse. The humans go into those showers, are cleaned, clothes removed, and then gassed to make them less aggressive when they are butchered."

"What?" I said in disbelief. "You led them to their deaths?" I remembered back to the gaunt woman who had died in the corral. But she was sickly. Why would the Overseers kill healthy people?

"Better them than me."

"How can you say that? My mother just went in there."

"She's already dead." The pet's tone was so neutral it was hard to believe what she was telling me.

"What happens to their bodies?"

"They are butchered for food."

I was speechless.

"Youngling, humans are gourmet food for the Overseers."

My stomach turned. The room spun, and I could feel myself getting faint. I fell over and clutched my stomach.

"How?" I said, sputtering.

"We are animals to them." Her response was so cavalier that I couldn't even respond.

I continued to lie on the floor until a moment later when Bejlae' arrived and took my leash. I looked at the other pet one last time as he pulled me out of the building. He yelled at me, but I didn't understand. The pain reverberated in my brain like a quivering bolt of lightning. He was making it happen. The snarl on his face showed me his rage and that he liked making me hurt.

Once inside, he took off my collar and pushed some buttons located on its inside before putting it back on my neck. Next, he took my leash and led me toward the door outside; when I reached the threshold, a terrible pain hit my head, and I could not go farther. He held me there for a few minutes, then let go of the leash, and I scurried back inside the house. I watched him with a wary eye; it's a good thing he didn't realize I knew how to take the leash off. Nevertheless, I knew I needed to be more careful about leaving the White Dome House in the future.

Once I was alone again, I felt for the small, indented button. But Bejlae' had done something, and pain ran the length of my arm every time I brought my hand close to the button. I could no longer release the collar without experiencing excruciating pain in my arm. I was a prisoner again.

Chapter 6

ξ

The Colonization

It was late evening and finally time for bed. Bejlae' had spent a long time snorting at Ki'ichpanil—all through dinner even. But when Ki'ichpanil went to sleep, it gave me access to the house again. I needed to see Barru.

I found him in the sitting room where the family spent a lot of their time.

"Did you know about what they do?" I accused him. His eyes were sleepy, and he folded his arms as I addressed him.

"Of course. I tried to warn you."

"But they eat us for food!"

Barru leaned forward. "They are superior beings to us. They are more intelligent; they have power and technology we can't comprehend. As I said before, we can't speak their language; our vocal cords won't even allow us to learn. But they don't understand our language either; to them, it probably sounds like different intonations of noise. They believe they are superior because they are."

"How long has this been happening?" I asked, sitting down and crossing my legs.

Barru cleared his throat. He kept his body facing away from mine, but he would look in my direction occasionally. "I don't know, but I have picked up a lot of information over the years. I once was a

Judas Goat, leading humans to the slaughterhouse. I did this for many of seasons before they let me retire, but because I was so loyal to them, they decided to bring me into the house. I have been their pet ever since."

"How could you do it?" I asked. Tears crept into the corners of my eyes.

"They trained me. They would have me lead herds from one pen to another until they got comfortable with me. Eventually, I was encouraged to lead them to the slaughterhouse, and I would be rewarded for doing my job. It wasn't until later I realized what was actually happening."

"I just don't understand any of it."

"About two hundred years ago, humans ruled this planet. We lived in cities; we farmed the land; we raised our own cattle for food. We are, after all, not so different from them. Except for a few slight differences. Where they are united by their technology, we fought each other all the time."

"We are nothing like them," I said, my eyes widening in disbelief.

He ignored me and continued. "Their cities were golden, and at first, many people thought the Overseers were gods come to Earth. When they made no attempt to communicate, our armies tried to conquer them, but we lost because our leaders squabbled over who would lead the attack. We fought wars over which country would align itself with the aliens. We were so arrogant, never realizing they thought we were herds of buffalo ripe for the harvest and nothing more. By the time we realized our weapons were useless against their technology, they decimated our capacity to fight back."

"How so?"

"We had missiles and bombs. But their force fields were not

damaged at all. Their Reaper-bots, now adapted to harvesting humans, are terrible weapons of war."

"Why didn't they just wipe our species out?"

"It was soon after that they started moving humans into the white-domed camps. Eventually, the entire human population had been transported to the camps. For hundreds of years, before they even arrived, the aliens were taking people and they did tests on them. Sometimes they even brought them back. But in the years just before the colonization, the aliens started eating human flesh. Many people went missing during those years. And so, when they colonized, they began farming us for food."

"But don't they know we are sentient beings, with feelings and thoughts, and language?"

"I don't think they care, even if they did."

"How come none of the herds know about this? How come they don't need to be dragged to the slaughterhouse kicking and screaming?"

Barru shrugged. "The Overseers are very smart about not letting on what's happening."

"But why don't the Judas Goats tell them?"

"The Judas Goats are loyal to the Overseers. I am loyal to the Overseers. They have given me a good life. You are luckier than most because you didn't have to earn your right to become a pet."

I felt dumbfounded. "So my friend Seffie will give birth to many younglings and then be killed for her labor?"

"Yes, that is how it is."

"But why was I picked? All I did was kick the bullaman and make him bleed."

"I don't know why you were picked," he said. "I know Ki'ichpanil wanted a female human. She is training you, maybe for the arena."

"The arena?" I asked.

"I don't know much about it. What I do know is the aliens are a complex society. There are some that treat us kindly. There are some that don't."

"As a society, do they control our whole planet?"

"Yes, their spaceships are cities unto themselves. Most of the aliens still live in those cities. There are twenty or so cities around the world. Or so I have heard. I suppose there could be more. These farms, however, they were built later, and so do not run on all the same technology that fuels their cities."

"Technology? Like what?"

"I don't think anyone really knows how their ships work. But the aliens seem able to communicate with each other telepathically. Their weapons seem controlled by their minds."

"Is that how they conquered our planet? With these telepathic weapons?"

"Their weapons do not destroy. Their weapons disable. Enemies disabled are more useful than enemies killed. The prehistoric humans had to fight by targeting the aliens. But the aliens only had to approach us. Their force field protected them from our weapons, and their ability to inflict pain disabled us. We lost quickly. I'm sure we didn't seem like more than wasps trying to fight them."

"Is there no hope for humanity then?"

"This is our reality, and we accept our reality; knowing the truth does not make the reality any different than what it is."

"How can you say that?"

"It is what it is."

Unable to spend even another moment with Barru, I stood up and made my way back to Ki'ichpanil's room.

She was sleeping soundly. I glanced down at the tablet she had been reading to me. I picked it up and brushed the surface over her hands, and it came to life. But I didn't recognize the images on the screen.

Cautiously, I moved her hand to the screen. The image changed again and what Ki'ichpanil had been reading to me flashed on the screen. The letters were foreign to me. I tried to remember what she had read, but I couldn't.

After dropping the tablet back where I had found it, I curled up and tried to sleep. I determined then I would learn to read their language. If I couldn't speak it, maybe I could learn to write it.

Part 2

The Wilderones

Chapter 1

ξ

The Hunters

Many seasons passed in the Overseer's home. During that time, I dedicated myself to learning the alien language. During the evening, when she read to me, I tried to follow along and paid close attention when words I recognized appeared in the text. Finally, after about four seasons, many words began to make sense. The first words I recognized were ones I was already familiar with. Whenever I heard her read *come* I looked where her finger was, and I memorized the script and the letters. *Stay* was the next word I learned. Then: *Dinner. Farm. Minotaur.* And on it went.

I still could not speak the language. It was too difficult to make the sounds of their unique phenomes with my limited vocal cords. But while the household slept, I would practice writing the letters and words on the palm of my hand.

I wasn't sure what I hoped to accomplish by learning their language. Still, I suppose, I hoped once they realized that we were intelligent and could communicate, they would change their ways and no longer see us as a food source.

I tried to keep track of time, and to my best recollection, I was in the Overseer's home for five years. And it took me that long to master their language.

I can remember the moment when I realized I could understand everything they said. I could write clear sentences with their lettering and follow their unique grammatical rules.

We were sitting around the family living area. Ki'ichpanil was on the floor with me curled up at her feet. Occasionally, she would pet my head.

Bejlae' turned to her. *"Ki'ichpanil, how was school today?"*

I glanced up at the sound of Ki'ichpanil's name. *"Well, Papa, we are learning about history, and about when the Minotaurs settled here. I asked my teacher if she thought we would ever go home."*

Turning my head, I listened intently. Bejlae' noticed me. *"No, my dear, this is our home now."* He kept his gaze firmly fixed on me. I glanced toward Ki'ichpanil, expecting her to respond.

"Hey, did you see that?"

"What, Papa?"

"Your pet, it's like she is listening to what we are saying."

Ki'ichpanil smiled. *"She does that all the time. I think she is trying to mimic our conversation."*

"Animals don't have a language," Bejlae' corrected her.

Ki'ichpanil petted my head again. *"I'm glad that you gave her to me."*

"Well, since she's so smart, maybe we should start teaching her to be a herder?"

"She could help round up some wilderones."

"Oh, you think so?" Ki'ichpanil seemed happy. *"Maybe we should take her hunting and see what she does."*

Wilderones was a term I had heard a few other times. I wondered if they were humans who didn't live in the white domes, the free ones, and weren't under the control of the Minotaurs. This was one of the tidbits of information I had picked up over the year.

I learned that they came from a distant planet, hundreds of millions of light-years away from Earth. Their civilization had completely taken over their planet, and it had reached its carrying capacity. A few explorers searched for other worlds that could support their massive civilization. Over a couple of hundred years—Earth time—they would arrive on various new planets, take samples, and return home. Finally, about two hundred years ago, the first settlement ship arrived on Earth. They built their first city.

They started farming humans soon after that. Much of the meat gets sent back to their home planet to feed their citizens.

I had also learned that billions of humans all over the Earth lived in white-domed farms. They kept us fed by taking the blood of our own dead, mixing it with grain, and feeding it back to us.

Ki'ichpanil continued speaking. *"I learned that when we first came here, we had to fight the humans, and they had weapons too."*

Bejlae' laughed loudly. *"Their weapons were the equivalent of a monkey throwing his own poop."*

Ki'ichpanil laughed.

I grunted with disapproval.

"I think we upset her," Bejlae' said, laughing again. "*Now, time for bed.*"

Ki'ichpanil stood and motioned for me to follow her. I stood and stretched my legs, then went after her. Bejlae''s gaze followed me out of the room. For the first time, I wondered if the Minotaurs knew we had language, and were sentient, but didn't care.

"I knew you were smart," Ki'ichpanil said, rubbing my head again. *"Tomorrow, I will take you hunting. It is so much fun. You will learn to be the best herder in the world."*

I wanted to ask what a herder did, but I suspected I already knew. There was no fucking way I would ever cause more humans to be taken into captivity.

An internal debate raged in my mind. I could let Ki'ichpanil know that I understood them. But was the risk of letting her know too great?

Ki'ichpanil fell asleep. And I made up my mind. I unlocked her tablet and wrote on a blank page, in their script:

I can understand you.

The door to Ki'ichpanil's room hissed open. Bejlae' didn't often come into her room. But for whatever reason, he decided to this night. He saw me holding the tablet and he bulled over to me and yanked it from my grasp. He didn't speak but read the screen.

He moved quickly. I felt a debilitating force press against my mind and his foot came down hard on my neck. He held me firmly to the floor.

Bejlae' bent down and spoke in a harsh whisper. *"This isn't your planet any longer. Tomorrow you will die in a hunting accident. It's too bad, since my daughter clearly loves you."*

He stood and left me on the floor. Pressing a button on a remote, I knew that he had locked the doors to the home. I had no chance of escape. I felt a pit in my stomach.

At dawn, he returned and woke Ki'ichpanil up. He attached the leash and clipped it to Ki'ichpanil's arm. *"Your human is all ready to go."*

"I hope she can learn to be a herder," Ki'ichpanil said.

Bejlae' did not respond as he led the way to the larger golden chariot. I stepped onto it behind Bejlae', and Ki'ichpanil stood behind me. Bejlae' made it move using his gold ring, and soon we were hurtling through the farm toward the northern gate.

The entire farm was covered by a translucent dome. I had never been outside it before, but Ki'ichpanil had taken me a couple of times to its edge, and I had felt it with my hands.

Today, the gate opened as if by magic, but I knew it was because of Bejlae''s ring.

Outside of the dome, the land was dry, decaying, and there was no sign of life nearby. I didn't know it at the time, but I would learn that the aliens sucked life out of the ground to energize their farms and cities. But a good distance away from the white domes, there was green and forested land.

We stopped at the edge of the forest. I had never seen anything so beautiful, and my heart cried out to be free in it. I felt like I was meant to be part of this nature.

Bejlae' handed my leash to Ki'ichpanil and told her to hang on tight. He then turned to the chariot and detached two drones from the side. The drones were cylindrical with wings on both sides, which had propellers on the tops and bottoms. They came to life when Bejlae' ran his gold ring over the red eye. It floated alongside Bejlae' with a whirring sound. Underneath them, I could see small, circular barrels.

Bejlae' ran his golden ring alongside one of the drones, and I watched as the drone mimicked all his movements. Where he looked, the drone looked. He was controlling it with his mind. He took a test shot and hit a tree with a dart that flew from the drone's barrel.

Ki'ichpanil ran her hand along the side of the other drone.

"Is her collar connected to both drones?" she asked.

"Yes," Bejlae' replied.

"So, what happens next? How will we know if she can be a herder?"

"It depends on how good she is at finding her own kind."

"I don't understand."

"The humans can sense each other in some way; they always

find each other. If she is good at finding her kind, we will follow above with the drones. When we find the herds of wilderones, then we can shoot and collar them. And remember, the drones only have a range of a few hundred feet, so we will have to run to keep up. That is what makes it so much fun."

"But could Kalaya get away?"

My ears perked up again.

"No," Bejlae' replied. *"The collar will keep her close. Besides, the drones stay with her, and there is nowhere she could go that they can't follow."*

Ki'ichpanil let go of my leash. At first, I just stood there, waiting. But a new feeling welled up inside of me, and I couldn't help myself; I felt free. I started to run. Even though I knew the drones were following me, I felt alone, like I was actually getting away from them. It was as if the past five years of being their pet, obeying their rules, was all behind me and I was running to a life without them. Fuck, it felt good.

The ground was rough in some places and soft in others; I tried to keep to the green grassy areas, and I ran—the sound of the drones humming constantly above my head.

A thought occurred to me: if I went into the forested areas, maybe I would escape the drones. But I would have to remove my collar. At least the Overseers didn't know I knew how to remove it.

The trees moved by me at a rapid pace. The smells of nature permeated my nostrils, and it was the most beautiful thing I had ever experienced; for the first time in my life, I felt alive.

Stopping, I knelt down and touched the ground. It was different than the dirt inside the farm; it seemed cleaner. I let the texture of it rub between my fingers.

The drones hovered just above me; suddenly, I felt a jolt of electricity in the collar. They wanted me to keep running. Standing, I once again ran.

The trees were old, and sparse vegetation grew on the forest floor. I had lost track of time when I came upon a rocky river. I stopped and looked over a ten-foot-high cliff. The drones stopped over me.

The drones could track me in the water, but maybe I could move fast and get out of range. They might not be able to catch up. Could my Overseers use the drones to kill or disable me if they thought I would escape?

I jumped off the cliff into the water. The drones hovered with me as I hit the water. The river was rapid, rougher than anticipated, and I kept getting pulled underwater. I wondered if this had been a terrible idea.

Each time my head crested the water, I sucked in air and looked around; I could see the drones still following me. I was moving fast, and I wondered if Bejlae' and Ki'ichpanil were worried. I shoved that thought out of my head.

The sound of rushing water ahead of me caught my attention, and it looked like the river just disappeared.

A moment later, I was swept over a waterfall. My arms and legs were flailing as I tried to fly, but the inevitability of gravity pulled me down. All I could see was the pool I was rapidly descending toward. There was only the briefest thought—*fuck*—as my feet struck the water and sunk into the deep pool.

This time, I felt like a weight was holding me under the water. I couldn't get to the surface, and I could feel the air rapidly leaving my lungs. This was it. I was going to die. But at least I'd had this briefest moment of feeling free. The unbelievable urge to breathe—to take in the air I knew wasn't there—was overcoming me.

Without warning, the current sucked me out of the pool, and I found myself spit up on a sandy beach behind the waterfall. Sputtering and coughing, I pulled myself onto the beach and just lay there, trying to regulate my breathing. I could see through the water—the drones were hovering just on the other side, the tracking device telling them precisely where I was.

Time. I was running short of it. I reached up and fumbled for the clasp. An excruciating pain ran down my arm. Grimacing with determination, I forced my hand to the small, indented button. The pain was unbelievable, but I bore it. Finally, my finger and thumb found the indent, and I pressed the button. The moment the collar clicked off my neck, the pain subsided.

I dropped the collar. A dart flew through the waterfall, but it fell harmlessly to the right side of me, just over where I had dropped the collar. I smiled. They knew I had removed the collar, but the drones were connected to the collar and not me specifically. I took a deep breath, dove into the water, and let the current pull me through the pool at the base of the waterfall.

Like fingers pulling a rope, the river took me away. My head crested the water briefly, and for the last time, I saw the drones waiting at the waterfall, evidently thinking I was still behind it.

Chapter 2

ξ

The Game of Hide-n-Seek

The river was violent and tumultuous. Each time my head went underwater, I thought it would be the last time, and that I would die before getting another breath of air. But then I would surface for another brief moment, gasping.

I turned myself in the water so my feet were in front of me; that way, I could see what was coming toward me.

Eventually, the current washed me over to a small pool on the side of the raging river, and I was able to splash toward the edge. I pulled myself up onto the rocks and lay there gasping for air, my body utterly spent.

A moment after I caught my breath, I heard the drones. They would find me soon if I didn't get off the riverbank. A dense forest of green leafy trees grew on either side of the river, and I hoped it would provide some protection.

Crawling on my hands and knees, I pulled myself into the underbrush. The forest was thick. Willows and small shrubs covered the ground, offering excellent protection for eyes flying above me. Finding a dense willow brush, I slid into its center. I could still see the edge of the river through the trees, and I hoped it provided enough cover. I prayed that I was hidden even with my limited understanding of their technology.

It was several minutes of tense waiting when I saw the drones fly by, following the path of the river. I thought maybe they would go right past me and miss me altogether. But that hope faded when the humming sound returned, as both drones stopped over the place where I had pulled myself from the river. They waited there.

My stomach growled in hunger, and I wrapped my arms around it to try and silence the noise.

The sound of voices hit my ears, and every nerve in my body strained to hear them. It was Bejlae' and Ki'ichpanil, and a moment later, they walked into my field of vision. Thankfully, they were on the opposite side of the river from me.

"She came out there," Bejlae' was saying. *"We need to find a way across the river. She is just over there on the other side. I can sense her."*

"Maybe get the drones to go a short way into the forest and see if they can pick up a trail?" Ki'ichpanil offered.

Bejlae' nodded.

I couldn't see a way to move without causing branches to stir.

Ki'ichpanil looked upset, and Bejlae' tried to console her. *"It's okay, Daughter; I will get you a new pet. But we have to make sure this one dies."*

"I'm sad we have to kill her, but I understand what you mean, Papa."

I glanced up into the sky. I could make out the white orb of the sun through cracks in the forest canopy. It was near midday.

Bejlae' and Ki'ichpanil continued to walk along the river until they disappeared from my field of vision again. The drones stayed on my side of the river. They spun and looked in different directions as various sounds caught their attention.

Very slowly, I turned around. The forest floor was thick in every direction, but I could see another dense willow just a few feet behind me. Maybe I could work my way from willow tree to willow tree?

Barely daring to breathe, I crawled like a crab, trying to keep my eyes on the drones. I couldn't see as clearly where I placed my hands, but I'd be fine as long as I didn't cause a branch to snap. The willow boughs parted as I left the safety of the tree. Immediately, the movement caught the attention of the drones, and I froze. Thankfully, a gust of wind rushed up over the river into the forest, causing other willow trees to move as well.

Feeling confident that the wind could help hide my movements; I moved a bit quicker. I didn't bother hiding in the nearby willow tree, but went farther back until I completely lost sight of the river. At least I knew that now the drones couldn't see me either. But I had no idea how long it would take Bejlae' and Ki'ichpanil to find a way across the river.

The farther I got from the river, the thinner the underbrush became. Most of the trees were tall aspens and cottonwoods, and there was no clear path through the woods. My pasty skin and white smock, however, didn't provide much in the way of camouflage.

I walked until the muscles in my legs started to feel tight. It had to be early in the afternoon, as I felt famished, but I didn't dare stop. I was deep into the woods now, and I hadn't seen any sign of other life since entering the forest. But my senses told me there were other life forms around.

Abruptly, the forest opened into a clearing, surrounded by trees. In the middle of the clearing stood a massive tree. Its trunk was so thick, ten people linking arms wouldn't be able to wrap it. It reached up into the sky. I would be able to see for miles if I climbed it. At the very least, I figured the aliens couldn't climb trees and I might be safer, higher up.

The tall grass brushed my legs as I ran. I didn't look back; I just ran until I reached the tree. Quickly, I turned my back and glanced around. Nothing was there.

The grooves in the bark were thick, and small notches that didn't appear natural circled the tree. It was a good fifteen feet up to the first set of branches. But using all the strength I could find, I clung to the grooves, dug my feet into the notches, and climbed up the tree.

Reaching the first large branch, I pulled myself up onto it and paused to catch my breath. The leaves were so thick I couldn't see very far. But it was easier to climb up from there.

About two-thirds of the way up the tree, I saw something interesting. The bark lapped over itself, and when I reached the branch it was next to, I could see that behind the fold was a hollowed-out section of the tree. I could slide behind it and hide.

The squeeze through was tight, but once I had entered the hollowed section, I paused. It wasn't empty.

A human skeleton along the side wall caught my attention first. It wore some rags of clothing, and I went over to examine them. They practically crumbled at my touch. This person had been dead for a long time.

Next to the pile of bones was a wooden chest, and I ran my fingers over it. I had seen similar things in the Overseers' white-domed house, so I knew what it was. Opening the latch, I lifted the lid. Inside were several other pieces of clothing, neatly folded tight. They did not crumble at my touch, even though they smelled ancient. I pulled out a leather jacket; but the sleeves were a bit too short for me, so I put it aside. There was a brown leather skirt under the jacket. I wrapped it around my waist. Then I saw the boots. I had never worn a pair, but I had seen the Overseers' footwear; these were different because they were made for humans.

I pulled them on. They too were a bit tight, but not so much my toes hurt. Walking around, I felt taller and better, like I was more of a person.

When I dug into the trunk, I found two more treasures: a hunting knife in a sheath and a wooden tube about the length of my arm, with carvings all over it. I put it up to my mouth and blew air through the end. Not sure what it was, I put it aside.

It was too bad that the black leather jacket was small. But it was only tight on my arms. I found a seam along the shoulder, and taking the knife, I cut off the sleeves. The jacket now fit perfectly, and it would offer some protection.

There were a lot of other treasures in the hollowed-out room. But the sound of drones humming interrupted my search.

I returned to the folded entrance and peeked out. Ki'ichpanil and Bejlae' were looking up from the base of the tree, and the two drones were hovering near their heads.

As the drones began their ascent, a reddish light emanated from their noses. I ducked my head back into the hollowed-out room and looked around wildly. Would they find the fold? My gaze rested on the wooden tube. It was very hard, and I didn't think it would break. I could hit the drones with it.

I needed a club. I ducked my head out again; the drones were still only about halfway up the tree. I touched the knife I had sheathed at my waist. I could stab the drones.

I ducked back into the safety of the room. If they found the fold, the drones could also squeeze through, but not easily. My best chance of defeating the drones would be to attack them one by one as they entered the tree. But that meant getting them to follow me in.

I half squeezed out of the flap and waited for the drones to see me. I heard Bejlae' yelp as soon as they did, and the machines flew straight at me. I was amazed at how quickly they moved. I had just managed to duck back into the room when I heard the sound of three darts striking the tree.

The drones slowed at the fold. I leaned against the wall, waiting for them to enter. The red light came first. But they weren't able to see me because the light couldn't bend around the corner. The drones would have to fly past me before they could see me.

The first drone's nose came through the opening. I waited, gripping the hunting knife with both hands. As soon as I saw the body, I brought the knife down into the top of the drone. There was a feeling of resistance, but then the knife slid through. I gave it a twist, and the drone dropped to the floor. Its light was out.

The second drone followed the other one in, and I was able to dispatch it just as quickly. I could hear Ki'ichpanil and Bejlae' speaking, and I went to the branch and looked down.

"She destroyed them," Ki'ichpanil said.

"But we know she is up there. I will call for assistance."

"But how did she know what to do?"

"Sometimes even animals get lucky."

I had no way to get out of the tree without them catching me. I looked around the room and wished for escape.

Chapter 3

ξ

The Plan of Attack

Light from the afternoon sun shone brightly through the flap, and I could see particles of dust floating around the room. The light itself came to rest on the wooden pipe I had found earlier.

I bent down and picked it up. It was a hollow wooden tube; what good would it do? How could I use it to help escape this trap?

The sound of one of the drones trying to start up again interrupted my thoughts. The reddish light on one of them, dimmer than before, was trying to reignite. Gripping the hunting knife, I went back over to it. Just as I was about to stab it again, there was a hissing sound, like a sharp outtake of breath. A moment later, a dart shot out of it and stuck into the opposite wall.

I didn't wait for the drone to fire another shot. I plunged the weapon over and over again into the body of the drone.

Then I fell to the floor and looked over the wreckage.

The drone had split in half, and bits of wires, plastic, and darts spilled on the floor.

After picking up one of the darts, I rolled it around in my fingers. Barru had said the aliens had technology that disabled their opponents; these darts must use that technology. I wondered if a single prick of the end would cause paralysis.

I didn't dare try it out.

But I considered that the darts would fit nicely into the

wooden pipe—almost perfectly, like the pipe had been carved to hold them.

The drones fired the darts by using air pressure. After placing the dart into the end of the wooden pipe, I blew air through it from the other end. Instantly, the dart flew from the tube and stuck into the opposite wall.

I could use this as a weapon. I wondered how far I would be able to shoot it, just using my breath alone. Loading a second dart, I went to the fold in the tree and, taking a deep breath, shot the dart. It flew about ten feet before dropping to the ground below. Bejlae' and Ki'ichpanil immediately examined the fallen object from the tree.

"What's she doing?" Ki'ichpanil asked her father.

"I'm not sure. Maybe just tossing out miscellaneous pieces from the drones."

"Do you think she knows the darts are coated with a disabling poison?"

"Shh," Bejlae' hushed.

Their conversation fell to a whisper. But it didn't matter, because I didn't know how much time I had before other Minotaurs arrived. I was sure they would be here before nightfall. Night would have made escape easier. But I knew I wouldn't be given that luxury.

I returned to the trunk and dug through the remaining contents. I found a leather satchel, lying neatly on the bottom. The belt crossed over my body, and the bag rested on my hips. Ideal for holding the darts from the drones. I placed them into the bag. I had a total of fifteen projectiles, including the ones I had already shot and pulled out of the wall.

After loading one dart, I tucked the blowgun into my belt. I would need both hands to climb down the tree. To stay unseen, I would have to stay on the side farthest from Bejlae' and Ki'ichpanil.

I knew I would be able to manage.

I had to make a move soon. After rechecking all my supplies, I crawled out onto the limb just outside the fold in the tree. I could see the two Minotaurs waiting at the bottom; thankfully, they weren't looking up.

Flattening myself next to the tree, I started my descent. The finger and toe holds were narrow, and the boots, I found, inhibited my climbing—but I didn't want to remove them because they would help once I was on the ground.

Approximately halfway down the tree, I started to feel a sense of pressure surrounding me, and I stopped. It was like a thousand-pound weight pressing against my brain.

I had felt this sensation in the corral when the Overseers had used their force field on me. Judging the distance between the Minotaurs and my location, their force field seemed to extend about twelve feet. I wouldn't be able to jump twelve feet away from the tree. And even if I could, they were faster than me; there was no way I would get away.

There were no branches near me at this point, just the tiny finger and toe holds. But I couldn't go down any farther without risking the force field debilitating me. I would have to shoot them first.

I stayed on the opposite of the tree trunk from the two Overseers. They would see me when I moved, and my only hope was in their inability to reach me with the force field.

I took in a deep breath, and the aroma of the tree bark gave me hope. I took the first step around the side of the tree.

"Papa, look!" Ki'ichpanil yelled. *"She's climbing down."*

I stopped when I could see both of them.

"She has nowhere to go but back up," Bejlae' said.

I took the blowgun out of my belt and placed the end to my lips. I aimed with one hand; I clung to the tree like a gecko with the other.

"What's she doing?"

"I don't know," Bejlae' replied.

I blew out the end of the blowgun, and the dart careened through the air, striking Bejlae' directly in his stomach.

"Papa!" Ki'ichpanil yelled.

"Bitch!" he said. Then he collapsed to the ground.

Ki'ichpanil wasn't looking at me, and the force field weight disappeared. I realized they needed to focus to use the force field. I dropped to the ground, landing on my feet with a violent thud.

I shoved a dart into the end of the gun and blew it at Ki'ichpanil, striking her in the back. She turned to look at me, a stunned look in her large, round eyes. A moment later, she folded to the ground. Her horns hit the dirt and created a small crater.

I was unsure how long the poison would last, so I turned and started running for the cover of the trees. I made sure I was heading in the opposite direction of the river. I wanted to get deeper and deeper into the forest.

I had just reached the edge of the forest when I heard the humming sound of drones, and two more Minotaurs entered the clearing from the opposite side. I thanked the trees I had decided to flee when I did. But I didn't want to linger any longer.

As I ran, I felt my breath leaving me quickly. Unaccustomed to physical exertion, I knew I would not be able to keep up this pace for too long. I tried to maintain a slow jog through the woods.

It was nearing evening, and the sun had fully set when I heard the sound of a drone above the trees over me. I flattened myself next to a tree and waited. It was flying in a circular pattern, searching.

I hoped it would go away, but the sound kept getting closer. The only way I could think to escape was to try and get outside the circle closing in on me.

When the humming drone was once again behind me, I ran with all my strength to try and get past it. I reached a small rock hill in the forest, and I stopped. My gaze darted in every direction, like a buzzing black fly. But my hope was quickly disappearing.

A voice hissed at me.

"They're going to find you; get in here."

Relief! It was another human voice. I searched the rocks until I saw a dirty face staring out at me from within a tiny cave.

Ducking into the cave, I found another woman about my age. She was wearing blue pants and a black leather jacket. Her hair was black, and her skin was covered entirely in mud.

"There is a mudhole just over here," she said, motioning. "Cover yourself in it."

"Why?" I asked.

"Those drones are heat-seeking, and they will be able to spot you through the trees, if they haven't already. The mud and dirt also hide you from the Cabras's minds."

I had no idea what she was talking about. I took gobs of mud and rubbed it over all parts of my body.

"It might already be too late," she said. "If they know to look in this part of the forest, they will find us. Those fucking drones can see where we have walked."

"What do we do?"

"You can hide here as long as you like. But I'm getting the fuck out of here."

I liked her voice. It was husky and commanding. It made me feel instantly safe.

"I want to go with you," I pleaded.

"Not going to happen. I felt obliged to save you, but that's it. If we travel together, we risk being seen. Two are easier to track than one."

"But I have nowhere to go," I said.

"Go back to your tribe."

"I don't have a tribe."

She looked at me; her deep brown eyes trying to see into my soul. "What do you mean? No one out here is without a tribe."

"I lived in the white domes, but I escaped."

"Are you a fucking herder?" Her tone was sharp, and I could sense an edge of fear. She grabbed me by the back of the head and parted my hair to see the barcode imprinted there. "Fuck!"

"They wanted to make me one," I said. "But I got away."

"How did you do that?" She suddenly seemed very cautious of me.

"I swam down the river."

"Maybe they wanted you to get away so you could lead them straight to us." She cursed again.

"They didn't. I escaped. I even destroyed two drones"

Nodding, she leaned her back against the rock and pursed her lips in recognition of my feat.

"Very well," she said after a moment, but her back was rigid, and her fingers taut. "I will take you to my tribe. But they might not like you if they think you will betray us to the Cabras."

"Cabras?"

"It's what we call the aliens. It means goat."

I laughed and immediately clamped my hand over my mouth.

The woman smiled and then whispered. "My name is Sashim. What is yours?"

"I'm Zee."

I felt like I had closed my eyes for only a brief moment when Sashim touched my shoulder and I jolted awake, eyes wide.

She held in her hand a small, blue object. "Take this," she commanded.

"What is it?" I took it out of her hand.

"It's a pill. A drug. You need to swallow it. It will decrease Cabras's force field's ability to impact you. It'll feel heavy still, but you won't get the headache. It won't minimize the debilitating agent in the darts. You will still feel it, and they will completely immobilize you."

"So, how does it help?"

Sashim swallowed her own blue pill. "If you are captured, you must pretend the force field has affected you. Then when they come to put the leash on you, hit them right in the ring on their nose. It might shock them enough to give you a head start."

"Okay." I swallowed the pill. It was hard to do.

"Another thing," Sashim said. "If they find us, we need to separate. As I said before, two of us are easier to track than one." She paused. Then she said: "If we do get separated, follow the way Ursa Major is pointing."

I had no idea what she was talking about, so she took my hand and led me to the small cave entrance. Pointing, she showed me the Big Dipper. "The handle points the way. Follow it, and you will find a mine shaft. You will find more humans there."

I nodded.

"Okay. We need to move quickly now."

I slung the blowgun across my shoulders, then readjusted the hunting knife and satchel. Sashim watched me do this.

"You should keep a good hold on those tools. They are rare," she cautioned. "There are humans that might try and take them from you."

I nodded again and then followed her into the night. Our feet were silent on the forest floor, and I couldn't hear anything else. There was no humming of the drones and no sounds of Minotaurs—of Cabras—speaking. The world felt different than it had before. It was more muddled and my brain felt foggy. I wondered if it was a side effect of the pill Sashim had given me.

Shivers rippled over my back and stomach as I followed Sashim. The heightening of my senses was overwhelming and I felt anxious. I was about to tell Sashim how I was feeling when she raised her fingers to her lips, so I refrained. Because I wasn't watching where I was going, I stepped on a branch, and the loud crack echoed in the night.

Sashim froze and waited. I didn't move.

The moon had risen, and it gave us enough light to see shadows moving in the trees. I gulped.

Sashim squatted down, and I joined her. Her eyes wildly looked around. She whispered into my ear. "I think there are four of them out there."

I nodded. "But I can't hear anything," I replied quietly, straining my ears.

"Shh," she hushed. "We need to separate. Do what I said."

She stood and pointed at me to go the opposite direction she was heading. She raised her fingers to her lips as she disappeared into the trees.

I waited. I was all alone again, and I couldn't see or hear anything related to the Cabras.

Suddenly there was a loud commotion, and lights from two

drones lit the area Sashim had snuck into. The humming sound pierced the quiet of the night. I fought every urge to run; instead, I crawled toward a tree.

Sashim had been caught in the commotion.

Chapter 4

ξ

The Remnants

Slowly, I inched forward. When I saw a break in the trees above me, I would check my direction to ensure I was still on course.

Sashim had told me to find her tribe. But it was challenging to maintain a steady direction because I had to dodge looming trees, steep hills, and densely overgrown parts of the forest.

The first rays of dawn stretched across the sky when I came to the edge of the trees. The forest ended abruptly, like there was a force field protecting it from the deserted wasteland in front of me.

I exited the trees, feeling exposed. If the Cabras were anywhere nearby, the drones would pick me up in an instant.

The wasteland was just that: dead earth. There was nothing green, just dirt; it was like someone had wiped all the color out of the world.

In the distance, I could make out a giant metallic structure. It was black, with a long arm stuck in the air, and a cable hung from the end. Next to it was a wooden shack: a single-story building with dirty windows and dilapidated walls.

I figured the run across the wasteland to the shack would leave me exposed for a good amount of time. If a drone spotted me, I would be caught before I reached it.

Not knowing what else to do, I took a deep breath and plunged forward. The boots offered some protection from the ground, which instantly became hard, rocky clay dirt. I was thankful for the footwear, which helped keep my balance easier as the dips in the ground would otherwise have caused me to lose my balance or sprain an ankle.

As I ran, the sun crested a dirt hill and the full force of its heat and light overwhelmed me, making it difficult to see. I lost sight of the shack for a moment, but by shielding my eyes with my hand, I located it again.

With a renewed burst of speed, I hurtled as fast as I could over the ground.

As the shack loomed in front of me, I heard the sound of a whip cracking in the air. A rope encircled my legs, dropping me to the ground. My face hit the dirt, and the foul taste of mud filled my mouth.

The fine black dirt filtered up my nose, and I sneezed loudly to clear it.

When I looked up, three bullaman were standing around me. At least, they looked like bullaman. They wore army fatigues, helmets, and marching boots not unlike mine.

"Take her inside," the first bullaman ordered. His face was dirty, like he had been wandering the wasteland for a long time.

The other two grasped me roughly under the arms. I was somewhat conscious of their hands touching the sides of my breasts, but I didn't say anything; I just felt awkward.

Half pulling, half dragging me, they took me into the shack. The first one pointed his black weapon at me.

"Who are you?" he asked gruffly, taking off his helmet. His brown hair was dirty and dusty. He gave it a shake.

"Are you Sashim's tribe?" I asked.

"Who are you?" he repeated sternly. I heard a clicking sound come from each of the weapons.

My gaze darted around the room, then from face to face of each bullaman. The shack was dusty, and it stank like the corral had stunk. There were two beds that looked slept in on one side of the wall, and there was also a door leading to another room.

"My name is Zee," I said. "But you have to help Sashim; she was captured."

"And what? You want me to go out to find her and fall into your trap, too? Fucking herder!" He grabbed my head and looked at the barcode on the back of my neck.

"Trap?"

"We've seen this before; the Cabras using humans to lure us into their traps."

"I'm not a herder," I pleaded. "I'm just trying to get away from them."

"So, you admit you are with them!" he said triumphantly.

"I was one of their pets. I used to be in the corrals."

"She's a heifer," another bullaman said. "She's only good for breeding."

"You have to save Sashim. She rescued me."

The leader motioned to another of the bullaman. "Go check it out."

The bullaman nodded and exited the shack. The crunching of his feet on the dirt disappeared as he ran toward the forest.

"Now, what are we going to do with you?" the bullaman leader asked himself. His hands ran over my entire body. They stopped at my belt, and he took out my hunting knife.

"Nice knife."

"It's mine," I declared. "You can't have it."

"What the fuck you going to do about it, heifer?"

He slid the leather satchel off my shoulders, then dug through it and pulled out the darts. "How did you come by these?"

"I destroyed a drone," I spat.

"You? No one has destroyed a drone. At least, not without a gun."

He turned me around and took my blowgun. "What's this? You play the flute or something?"

"Please give my things back," I pleaded. "I need them."

I tried to wriggle my hands free from the bonds that held them, but I couldn't. These bullaman knew what they were doing.

Trussed up and tossed into a corner, I watched the two remaining bullaman.

"How did you get out, bullaman?" I asked him suddenly.

"I'm a what now?"

"A bullaman."

He laughed. "Well, I guess you would see me as one. But I am an old-fashioned man."

My ears caught the distinction.

"I am freeborn and have never been a prisoner to the Cabras. We have a few that are."

The other man laughed. "Maybe she wants to bear your seed, Mert."

My eyes flared dangerously. I had kicked the bullaman and made him bleed; I'd do the same to this man. "I don't want to bear anyone's seed," I declared. "And I'll fucking kill anyone who tries."

The one called Mert laughed. "You mean you'd try."

The men sat down at a rickety desk, content to leave me alone. On it was a device similar to the tablets the Minotaurs had. Both men were watching it intently.

"What are you doing?" I asked. "What is that?"

Mert turned to me. "You've never seen a tablet before?"

"I've seen them. But what are you doing on that one?"

"It controls our security system. We must be vigilant in identifying threats to our tribe."

"I'm not a threat."

"We'll see."

I was ignored as they waited for the third man to return.

It was close to midday when I finally heard the crunching of his feet on the dirt. He poked his head in before entering the room.

He spoke in hushed tones to Mert. Mert glanced over at me. "You're sure?"

The other man nodded.

Mert came over to me and pulled me to my feet. "He found Sashim. Four Cabras are holding her captive. But they haven't moved on; from what Garetti can gather, they are searching for something. You, I think."

"What are you going to do?"

He smirked, and I didn't like its look. "Trade you for her."

"How? You can communicate with them?"

"Nope. Can you?" he asked.

I thought about my answer. If I admitted to being able to communicate, they might think I was working with them, and then they would just kill me. "No," I lied.

"I think we'll just throw you into the camp, and while they capture you, we'll free Sashim."

I sputtered while trying to respond. He pulled out a small gun. "This is a handgun. It shoots bullets, which are deadly. They'll kill you. So, don't even think about escaping."

He jammed the handgun into my back and pushed me forward. "No talking or you are dead. Understand?"

I nodded.

"Remnants, let's go!" he ordered the others.

Chapter 5

ξ

The Rescue

Mert brought us to the edge of a bluff overlooking the small encampment of Minotaurs. There were four of them, and each had a small tent set up. I immediately recognized Bejlae and Ki'ichpanil; I didn't know the other two.

"Sashim told me they could sense us. How come they can't right now?"

Mert touched the dirt covering his body. "The dirt is a shield. The density in the dirt makes it hard for them to see into our minds." He touched his fingers to his lips.

Two drones hovered just over their camp, keeping a watchful eye. In the center of the camp was a portable cage the Minotaurs had constructed, with Sashim in it. She looked absolutely disconsolate.

Mert backed us about fifty yards away from the cliff, keeping his handgun trained on me the entire time.

"It is clearly a trap. The moment we enter the camp, those drones will get us."

"Why don't you just take out the drones?" I asked sarcastically.

"Because the only way to get them is to shoot them. And if we open fire, the Cabras will use their weapons on us."

"There are only two drones," I defended. "I took out two drones by myself."

"The drones aren't our biggest threat," he said irritably. "We can take them out, but the aliens have their force field to defend themselves."

"Why don't you just shoot them, too?" I asked.

"Bullets don't harm them."

"What do you mean?"

"To the best of our understanding, they don't even have blood. We have no idea how to locate their hearts."

"So, shoot them in the face."

"Their skulls are impervious to bullets. But if we shoot them anywhere else in their bodies, the bullets just go in, and they pull them out without injury."

My mind went back to my escape from the tree. I said, "I shot them with darts and it knocked them out. Those darts are filled with some kind of paralytic."

He looked interested. "But with the drones, there are six of them and only three of us."

"There are four. Let me help you. Give me back my weapons and satchel. I can shoot the Cabras for you. Two of you can take out the drones from atop the bluff, and then you can rescue Sashim."

"You can hit all four of the Cabras?" he asked.

"I can get three of them. The fourth is just a child, and I don't think she will fight us."

"Which one is the child?" Garetti asked.

"The smaller one," I said, unsure why he would care.

"Okay," Mert said. His eyes narrowed and he looked at Ki'ichpanil. "Garetti, Malak, you guys get the drones from the bluff. Zee and I will enter the camp. She'll shoot the aliens, and I'll rescue Sashim." His face darkened, and he turned to face me, speaking to the other men. "If she betrays us, and I am captured, make sure you kill her," he ordered.

The two other men nodded and moved toward the edge of the bluff.

"Wait," I said.

They paused.

"Don't shoot the drones until I have taken out one of the guards." I knew I needed to hit Bejlae' first; he was the one I considered the greatest threat.

Nodding, the two men slunk off toward the bluff's edge.

"Come on," Mert said. He kept his handgun out, but he wasn't pointing it at me. "We have to move slowly and quietly. The drones have acute hearing, and will attack the moment they see us. They move quick and shoot faster. You need to be accurate, and quick, too."

He passed me my hunting knife, blowgun, and satchel. I loaded the gun and held two darts in my hand, ready to reload.

Each step we took was determined and purposeful.

I tapped Mert on the shoulder when we reached the edge of the camp and waited in safety behind a thick bush. With one finger, I motioned for him to go around the camp until he was behind a tent. I would go the other way to get behind Bejlae', who was sitting next to Ki'ichpanil. All of them seemed suddenly on high alert. It was like they could sense we were out there. My mind strayed back to the corral. Mentally kicking myself, I focused again. Now was not the time to be distracted.

Mert nodded to me and moved off into the night.

I glanced up at the drones. They were hovering about fifteen feet above our heads. They would spin to focus on different sounds in the trees around us.

Letting out a shallow breath, I crawled around the outer edge of the camp. I was surprised that Bejlae' had brought Ki'ichpanil out with him to the woods for the night. But maybe he considered it some kind of training for her. He liked to hunt.

I hoped Garetti and Malak were in position. Raising the blowgun, I aimed it at Bejlae'. I wondered if he had his force field up. I couldn't feel the pressure in my head, or the paralysis.

After I blew hard on the end of the blowgun, there was a subtle *woosh* and the dart fired through the air, hitting Bejlae' directly in the neck. I reloaded the dart gun and blew again, hitting one of the other Cabras. Reloading a third time, I fired, but the last adult Cabra was too far away from me, and the dart fell short.

The drones sensed the attack and moved into position.

I reached into the satchel and pulled out another dart as I ran a few steps toward the third alien. Dropping to a knee, I fired. Just then, I heard two loud bangs; they were like sharp cracks but far more ear-shattering. Both drones above my head burst into flames and dropped from the sky.

Ki'ichpanil was standing next to her father when she saw me.

My third dart hit the alien squarely on the chest, and it dropped to the ground, paralyzed.

Ki'ichpanil raised her golden ring and took a step toward me. *"Bad girl. Bad. Put it down."*

I felt the pain in my head start, but it was duller.

I loaded the blowgun. Behind me, Mert entered the camp and rushed toward the cage holding Sashim. It distracted Ki'ichpanil briefly.

Pointing the blowgun at Ki'ichpanil, I hesitated. Trying desperately, I formed some of the sounds of their language, and I said hesitantly, *"Go."*

Ki'ichpanil shook her head in disbelief. *"Are you trying to speak to me?"*

She took another step toward me. I couldn't let her get any closer or she would be able to use her force field on me.

I fired the dart, and it struck Ki'ichpanil in her hip. Immediately, she dropped to the ground.

Mert and Sashim appeared next to me.

"There is something to you," Sashim remarked. "I can believe you destroyed drones all on your own. Thanks for helping rescue me."

A moment later, Garetti and Malak also arrived.

"We need to get moving," Mert said. "How long will they be paralyzed for?"

I shook my head. "I don't know."

Malak took a knife from his belt and approached each of the aliens. I looked away in horror as he cut the gold rings off each of their fingers. He had to slice their skin around the edge of the gold ring to slide them off. I could see the look in Bejlae''s eyes when Malak took his ring. The alien might have been paralyzed, but he knew what was happening.

"Don't cut Ki'ichpanil's," I said.

"Who?"

"The child."

"Sorry, but this tech gives the aliens power. I will not let her keep it." He cut it off her finger.

"Bring her along," Mert suddenly ordered. "They take us captive; our scientists can learn a lot from this young one."

"I think it's a bad idea," I said.

"No one asked your opinion," Mert replied.

"Bejlae' will never stop looking for her."

"Then we better make sure he never finds her."

I felt despondent as I followed the four other humans back into the forest, Garetti and Malak pulling Ki'ichpanil by her legs.

"Keep a dart ready, should she start to come out of the paralysis," Mert ordered me.

I kept looking down at Ki'ichpanil as we walked. Her eyes looked sad. She was being taken away from her family. But then again, she had taken me away from mine without caring about my feelings.

When we reached the shack in the wasteland, we paused while Malak got the pulley system ready. I watched in fascination as an elevator arrived from a pit; we were going to go underground.

"Hey!" Garetti said suddenly. "Her leg just twitched!" He pointed at Ki'ichpanil.

"Shoot her again," Mert ordered.

I hesitated.

"Do it, or she will cause the death of us all."

I fired again. How were we any different than the Minotaurs? Fear welled up in my heart.

Part 3

The Wilerlands

Chapter 1

ξ

The Queen

Garetti and Malak pulled Ki'ichpanil's motionless form onto the elevator platform.

"It's about a hundred feet down," Mert announced, pressing a button on the control box next to him. "It doesn't go very fast, and it is dark."

I nodded.

As we descended, I felt a sense of panic that reminded me of being in the corral. The walls were tight. I couldn't see any of the others, and I feared Ki'ichpanil's paralysis might wear off.

"The thickness of the dirt makes us all but invisible to the Cabras," Mert offered. "It is why all human settlements are underground now."

After a few minutes, the space opened up, and a bit of light allowed me to see my surroundings. The elevator shaft opened into a massive underground cavern. It looked like a city that had been buried under a hundred years of rubble. Shops opened into the buildings that seemed almost built into the dirt. People were in windows in upper levels of the underground buildings. Some worked on wires that provided lighting to the entire cavern.

"How many humans live here?" I asked Mert.

He glanced at me. "There are about ten thousand of us in this hive."

"Hive?"

"Our cities are similar to ant hives. This is the main square."

"Are there other cities? Do you interact with them?"

Garetti smirked. "Sometimes, with the barrel of a gun."

"You fight each other?"

"Of course," Mert replied. "The Cabras aren't our only concern. Other tribes will attack and try to steal our goods. It happens all the time."

"Where do all the goods come from?"

"We have some scroungers who hunt the destroyed cities, finding all kinds of treasures, like books, weapons, and tech."

"How do the tribes attack each other? There is no way an army of humans can travel above ground unseen."

"They don't," Mert said. "We have built a massive network of roads to get to the deserted cities of *before*. The ancients also had underground transports." He paused like he had said too much.

"I don't understand. Wouldn't an attacking tribe just wipe you out and kill everyone?"

"Hardly," he said. "They only want to steal supplies: food and weapons."

"Do the people ever get to go above ground?"

Mert shook his head. "Only a few of us guards and scroungers."

The elevator platform came to a jarring halt at the head of the square. Buildings surrounded us. We stepped off. Immediately, a crowd of people surrounded us. Some of them reached out and touched Ki'ichpanil as we walked through the throng. I could see Ki'ichpanil's eyes moving from side to side as she tried to take it all in.

We came to a halt before a raised dais. On it stood a woman

at least twice my age. She had blond hair and wore a leather jacket and pants, along with steel-toed army boots. She had a scar on her right cheek.

Two guards stood next to her, with guns similar to Garetti's and Malak's.

"Her name is Queen," Mert said, keeping his gaze fixed on her. "She is our elected ruler."

One of her guards seemed familiar. Then it dawned on me; he looked a lot like the bullaman I had kicked and made bleed. He had black hair, bushy black eyebrows, and a black beard. He was tall, with solid muscle.

Sashim saw where I was looking. "That is Jenga."

"He looks like a bullaman," I said.

Mert smiled. "He used to be one. He was part of a farm in the white domes nearby. But the Cabras sold Jenga to another farm, and while they were transporting him, we rescued him and a whole bunch of others."

"Rescued? When?"

"Jenga was rescued about five years ago," Sashim replied.

I made a mental note to stay as far away from Jenga as possible. I didn't want to have anything to do with a bullaman. But even as I thought it, I kept glancing up at him.

"We rescue nucksa and heifers, too."

"Why do you still call them that? It's what we call them in the corrals."

"Because that is what they are," Mert said. "Most of them are so brainwashed they don't understand a life of freedom. They don't even understand simple social norms, like consent."

"That's awful."

"Not all of them, of course. Some of those we rescue easily fit into our society. We don't call them nucksa or heifers.

"The nucksa and heifers who don't want to join our society with a job all live down that tunnel." He pointed. "It is just a regular orgy down there."

The clamoring of voices ceased as Queen raised her hand. Every face looked at her.

"Why have you brought a Cabras here?" she demanded loudly.

Garetti and Malak dragged Ki'ichpanil up to the platform as Mert and I followed.

"Queen," Mert said. "We captured her and thought our scientists might want to take a look at her." He dumped the four gold rings into her hand. "We also took these from her and three others."

She looked impressed. "How is it you managed to capture this creature and take their rings?"

"She helped," Sashim said, nodding to me. "I found her in the forest while I was on reconnaissance. But the Cabras managed to capture me, and she helped Mert and the other Remnants rescue me."

Queen turned to face me. She squinted. "Do you trust her?"

Sashim nodded. "I don't think she's working for them."

"How did she help rescue you? Only one of their pets would know how to get around their technology."

She turned to me. "Have you managed to get the Remnants to bring the Cabras here so the others will search to rescue her?"

"I haven't," I said, matching her gaze. "I used to be her pet. But I escaped."

Queen raised her eyebrows. "A pet. We don't like the pets here." She glanced down at Ki'ichpanil. "Why isn't she moving?"

"She has been struck by a paralysis dart," I said. I unslung my blowgun and took a dart from my satchel.

Jenga's gun raised and pointed at me as I did it.

Queen raised her hand. "Show me." She pointed at a target; it was another woman about ten feet away from me.

"Her?" I asked.

"Yes."

"I can't," I said. "I can't do it to another human being. You can see the effects of the dart because the Minotaurs is still under its effects."

Queen's eyes narrowed again; she didn't like being disobeyed. "Take it to the scientists," she said. "I want to know as much about their biology as possible. If we can learn how to kill them, we might be able to defeat them."

"You've never killed one before?" I asked. It stunned me to think this was the first Minotaur they had ever been this close to or been able to study.

"We have never killed one," she said. "We run and hide. We don't fight them."

Ki'ichpanil started moving her mouth, and her snout twitched like she was trying to smell.

"She's coming out of the paralysis," I said. I could tell she wanted to fight back. There was a fire in her eyes.

Ki'ichpanil spoke to me in her grunts and snorts. *"Why am I here?"* Her tone was distinctly fearful. Maybe I had mistaken the fire for fear.

Queen laughed. "What's she doing? She must know we can't understand them."

I shrugged slightly. "She just wants to know why we have taken her from her father."

Queen turned her gaze to me again. Her eyes narrowed. "You

understand them?" she asked.

"Yes. I can understand their language."

"Can you speak it? How did you learn it? Did they teach you?" I could sense the accusation as she said it.

I shook my head. "I can only write it. I taught myself."

Queen snuffed her nose in disbelief. "You are becoming more and more interesting to me. You will have to teach me how to read it too."

"If you want," I replied. Maybe a small step in gaining acceptance with this hive.

"What is your name?"

"Zee."

"Well, Zee, you will go with Sashim and the Remnants. You can bunk with them. I will call you when I want to meet with you." She turned to Sashim. "Show her around, and make sure she knows where she is allowed to go."

After turning to walk away, Queen took several steps before stopping. "Zee, after you are settled, I'll send Jenga to escort you to the science wing. Our head scientist, Berner, will be very excited to meet you."

She turned and moved down the tunnel behind her, and the clamor of voices in the great hall reignited. Sashim touched my shoulder gently. I turned to follow, but not before I noticed Jenga's gaze still glued on me. At least his eyes were softer than those of the bullaman in the corral, I thought as I followed Sashim.

Chapter 2

ξ

The Knife Fighter

Mert, Garetti, and Malak took Ki'ichpanil away while Sashim led me down a different tunnel.

The room we entered was different than the cavern. It was built like a bomb shelter with bricks from floor to ceiling. Dug out in the wall were enclaves holding blankets and other personal items.

There were a hundred or so men and women huddled in different areas around small flames, cooking. The smell reminded me of dinners in Ki'ichpanil's home, when they cooked human flesh.

"What are they cooking?" I asked; I couldn't hide my tone of revulsion.

Sashim looked over at a group cooking over the small flame. "We usually eat a gritlike meal, similar to what you ate in the corrals. But sometimes, we go hunting and kill a pig or wild boar for food."

"You eat flesh?" I asked, horrified. Ever since I learned that the aliens ate human flesh, I couldn't fathom the thought of eating flesh.

"Of course," she replied. "But the pigs are only animals. They don't feel pain the same way humans do, and they don't think and live like humans do."

She spoke so nonchalantly about it. I was shocked. "How can you justify eating a living thing when you know what the Cabras do to us?"

Sashim shook her head. "It's different."

I knew I wouldn't be able to argue my point with her. I would never eat flesh.

Changing the subject, I motioned around the large brick room. "So, you are all the Remnants?"

"Yes," Sashim said. "We are the guards of our community." She pointed down a tunnel. "That leads to our training ground. We practice fighting by using hand-to-hand combat, and with weapons, like the guns you've seen. We also learn to fight with swords and daggers. As you were told before, we have to fight other hives. We tend to fight them using swords and knives; we have a stash of bullets for ammunition too."

"What do you use bullets for?"

"When we attack transports, we use them on the Cabras. They also destroy drones."

"But Queen said you've never killed one before?"

"Our bullets don't seem to do much damage to their bodies. But they do slow them down."

I raised an eyebrow. "How?"

"We don't know. It's one reason your Ki'ichpanil is so valuable; we might be able to learn why the bullets don't cause them to bleed to death, and find out where to shoot them to kill them."

"Are they going to kill Ki'ichpanil?" I asked.

"Eventually, yes. Berner will want to do an autopsy on the body to learn about their organs and other insides."

We stopped in front of an enclave in the wall with three bunks.

"This is me," Sashim said. "You can have the top bunk. No one is there."

"Okay, how do I get up?"

Sashim laughed, a single, loud coughlike sound. "You pull yourself up."

No problem.

"Now, let me show you the training grounds."

Since I didn't want to leave my satchel, knife, or blowgun, I followed Sashim out of the room, with all my stuff.

The tunnel leading to the training grounds was short, and at the end of it, a wooden door opened into an arena. Twenty or so men and women were fighting with various weapons on the main floor.

Loud bangs startled me; they echoed in the brick room. I jumped to the side of Sashim, my eyes wide in terror. Unconsciously, my hand went to the knife at my belt.

Sashim pointed to the side of the room as another volley of gunshots rang out and I saw more men and women shooting the guns at targets.

Across the room, a table caught my attention. I walked over and saw several knives lying on it. They each had different kinds of handles and blades. Some of the blades were shorter, and others were longer, with devilish black handles.

I pulled out my hunting knife and compared it to the others.

"Nice blade," a voice said to my left. Looking up, I saw Jenga's gaze on me. I recoiled slightly; he reminded me so much of the bullaman who had tried to inseminate me. Yet there was something different too.

"Thanks," I responded hesitantly.

"Are you any good with it?"

"I don't know," I replied.

"Well, do you have any idea how to use it?"

I smirked. "The sharp end goes into your enemy."

"It's a bit more complicated than that," he replied. I liked the tone of his voice. It was deep, but there was a timidity to it, which softened his overall demeanor. He was definitely not the aggressive bullaman I had been expecting.

Mert interrupted, having recently arrived from dropping off Ki'ichpanil. "Don't let him teach you knife fighting. If you want to learn, you learn from me."

Jenga's entire body stiffened, and his lips creased into a thin line. I was unsure why they didn't like each other—some toxic alpha male thing maybe.

Mert continued unabated. "In a knife fight, you want to target the three main areas that will inflict the greatest harm." He pointed to my neck, my chest and ribs, and then my inner thigh.

"Why?"

"Because it will cause your enemy to bleed out quickly. You never want to be in a knife fight long."

"That I agree with," Jenga interrupted.

Mert huffed, "You wouldn't go for the main arteries to disable and kill your enemy?"

Jenga picked up two training knives. They had been carved out of wood, but they looked like they could still do damage. "You talk a good game, Mert, but how about you and I spar?"

"Okay, let's go."

As they prepared to spar, Remnants from various nooks and crannies surrounded us. I could hear murmurs about who would win; there may even have been some betting going on.

Each man held his weapon differently. Mert held the wooden knife in a reverse grip, and his elbow was up like he was ready to punch just as quickly as jab the knife. Then he spun it on his hand, and it seemed like magic. I wasn't sure how he accomplished it, but it was fast and the blade reversed in his grip. Then he did again. He could transition quickly between a jab or stab.

Jenga held the practice knife in front of him. He took random swipes in front of his body. He held up his left arm, the one not holding the knife, so his open hand was just in front of his neck.

Mert held his left hand in an “L” shape from his body, using his forearm as a shield. His knife hand was static, ready to strike.

The fight started, and the men circled each other, each taking a step forward, giving a mock jab, and then quickly backing away.

Sashim leaned close into me. “If you lose a knife fight, you are dead. If you win a knife fight, you’re seriously injured.”

“Nobody wins in a knife fight,” Jenga said, keeping his vision fixed on Mert.

Jenga seemed much more relaxed than Mert, his gaze focused but almost lazy. He kept moving his knife hand in random swipes.

Suddenly Mert attacked with a jab for Jenga’s neck. Jenga countered quickly, and his practice knife struck the inside of Mert’s forearm.

Even though they used practice knives, the slice left a red welt. Mert struck again and again; clearly, he thought offense was the best course of action. But Jenga hung back, content to inflict smaller gashes on Mert’s arms and sides.

I could tell Mert was getting more frustrated as he could not penetrate Jenga’s wavering knife, which acted like a shield.

The fight ended quickly when Mert made a fatal error and overextended his reach on a strike for Jenga’s ribs.

Quickly, like an arrow released from a bow, Jenga’s knife struck Mert’s chest. It would have penetrated deeply had Jenga not pulled back at the last second.

“You’re dead,” he announced, tossing the knife to the

ground.

Mert had a murderous look on his face.

Jenga approached me. “You see, the three zones Mert was telling you about are important for the kill strike. But you only should use them once your enemy is tired and weakened by blood loss from numerous other strikes.”

Jenga glanced back at Mert. “In a real fight, each time I sliced his forearms and sides, he would have become increasingly disabled. Knife cuts hurt. If I was lucky, one of my strikes might have severed a nerve, and then my enemy would be incapacitated.”

I nodded in understanding.

“Most knife fighters wear protective forearm shins. They help prevent the slices of a knife in a fight. However, they can be bulky and often do not protect the backside of the forearms.”

I glanced at Mert, who was rubbing his hand over his forearms. There were red welts all over them, on both sides.

Taking my knife out of its sheath again, I felt the blade. “Would you teach me to use this?” I asked Jenga.

“Of course,” he replied without hesitation. “Your training can begin right after you visit with Berner. He is our scientist and he is excited to meet you.”

Chapter 3

ξ

The Scientist

Ki'ichpanil stood in a metal cage, wholly stripped of clothing. The bars surrounded her, reaching from ceiling to floor. She looked despondent, but she could move once again, which meant the debilitating dart's paralysis had worn off.

A man much shorter than me stood in front of her. He had to be just under five feet tall. His head was bald, with black hair on the sides that came to a ponytail at the back of his neck. He held in his hand a small recording device, which he spoke into.

"The alien female's features are similar to those of all the Cabras. Her neck is humanlike. Small horns protrude from her forehead. Nose is distinctly bovine in shape, but teeth are razor sharp." His voice sounded like he had a sinus cold.

As he spoke, Ki'ichpanil's eyes twitched. Her face was pale, and she looked like she was going to vomit. Although I could not recall ever seeing any of them get sick before.

"Her mammary glands are just beginning to develop, which suggests this Cabras is prepubescent. Her legs are covered with coarse hair, but her genitals are oddly humanoid," he said.

His eyes brightened at the sight of me. "Berner," he said, holding out his hand to me while he switched off the recording device.

"Zee," I said.

When I spoke, Ki'ichpanil looked up. She was very sad.

"I am fascinated," Berner said. He walked back over to the cage. "I knew their knees bent opposite than ours, very much like the hindquarters of a goat—I couldn't have asked for a better specimen."

I shrugged.

"And look here," he said, pointing without getting too close. His finger directed me to the area just behind Ki'ichpanil's head.

"This is some kind of bone plate that protects the neck; it comes down over their shoulders. It is fascinating; it protects their heads and upper chests. And their skin looks so much like ours, but it is thicker and harder to penetrate."

"Queen said I was to ask her questions?" I offered, not caring to hear more description of Ki'ichpanil's body, which kept me focused on her nakedness.

Berner's tone got even more excited. "Tell me how you learned to speak their language."

"I don't speak it," I admitted quickly. "I understand what they say, and I can write it, but I cannot say the words."

"Fascinating." His eyes glowed in wonderment. "Yes, we have some questions. So many. Like what are their bodies like inside? How do they procreate? Do they even see in color like us?"

I stared at him. "She's quite young," I told him. "I don't know if she can tell you everything."

"But I'm sure she knows how their species makes children and such," he said.

I sighed loudly. "Do you have something I can write on?"

He handed me a tablet.

I wrote: *Ki'ichpanil, I can understand everything you say. I can't speak your language, but I can write it. You taught me.*

Her eyes widened as she read what I wrote.

There was a catch of emotion in her tone. *"What have you done to me?"* she asked. *"I feel like I am dying. You must give me back my ring, my gold ring. I can only survive for a few days without it."* Her tone shifted, and I was intrigued. Was she lying?

I turned to Berner and repeated what she had said. His eyes sparkled, and he walked over to the table and picked up one of the four gold rings lying there. "Ask her what they are."

After writing down the question, I showed Ki'ichpanil. She refused to speak about them. So, I added, "Tell me what they are, and I might be able to get the scientist to give yours back."

Ki'ichpanil seemed to consider it. *"They are given to us when we are born,"* she said. *"They become part of us, and allow us to control our world with our minds. They are like antennae, extending our telepathy."*

I repeated her response to Berner. "I don't think she is telling us everything," I told him. "I think she only said anything because I told her I would try to get hers back to her."

Berner approached me. "Write this: You can have it back after you answer my questions."

Ki'ichpanil read the statement. *"What does he want to know?"*

"She'll do it," I told Berner.

"Where are they from, and why did they come here?" asked Berner. I wrote down his question and showed it to Ki'ichpanil.

She replied: *"Our home planet is six hundred and sixty-seven million light years away from here. But our civilization figured out how to jump through holes in space. When the Minotaurs found this planet, we realized the resources were plentiful enough to keep our home planet alive for thousands of years.*

"But the animals that controlled this planet—you humans—

needed to be pacified."

I wrote to her: "We aren't animals. We are sentient, with critical and creative thoughts, with feelings and emotions."

Ki'ichpanil shrugged, as if she was completely indifferent to this information. I would have thought she might be at least a bit intrigued. It began to reinforce in my mind the notion that they might in fact know the truth—that humans are sentient.

"I've only known you as animals. I am surprised we can communicate," she said.

"I learned from you reading to me and writing on your tablet."

"Does my papa know you can understand us?"

"Yes, I told him just before you took me out hunting. He told me he was going to kill me. He wanted to keep this a secret from you."

I sensed Ki'ichpanil did not like that answer.

"I want to go home," she pleaded with me. *"Wasn't I good to you?"*

After thinking for a moment, I responded: "You treated me like an animal. On some level, we are all animals, but all life should be considered equally valuable."

"What are you talking about?" Berner interrupted.

"She's just a child, and she wants to go home. I don't think she will tell you any more today. Will you give her gold ring back?"

"No, I will not," he said, turning from her and taking the ring to the table.

"Why not?"

"Because she told us that it helps extend her telepathic communication. If we give her the ring, an army of Cabras will descend upon us."

I was silent for a moment. "We can never let her go, can we?"

Berner shook his head. "We can't risk her telling her father about our civilization. They will butcher all of us. They are not a species that shows mercy—especially since we haven't been able to do research like this before."

"I'll talk to her for a bit more and see what she can tell me."

I returned to Ki'ichpanil's cage. "Are you my enemy?" I wrote.

"You were my pet. I cared for you, until you ran away."

"I don't think they are going to let you live unless you tell me everything. I need to know what your bodies are like, how you communicate with each other, and what can kill you. Like, why does the poison from the paralysis dart affect you?"

Ki'ichpanil was hesitant, and she talked slowly.

"We don't have bodies like you," she said. *"All of our major organs: heart, lungs, stomach, liver—kind of—are located behind a protective bone that runs over our heads and shoulders. It protects us from most weapons."*

"Do you have blood?"

"Yes, but not like humans. We do still need oxygen to survive, just like you. However, our major arteries and veins are inside our bones. Our bones are very strong, and are not easily penetrable by anything on your planet. But oxygen is brought to our skin by millions of little capillaries; they immediately seal off and collapse if they are injured. That is why your weapons do not harm us. But the paralysis darts do, because the paralysis poison and dart doesn't hurt the capillaries. From there, the poison can spread quickly throughout our bodies."

"So the only way to kill your kind is by poison?"

"Yes, but there are only a couple of things on your planet that would poison us and kill us. And I don't know what they are."

I decided I wouldn't tell Berner what I had just learned about how they could be killed. If I could protect Ki'ichpanil, maybe they would grow to like her, maybe as a pet. Eventually, they might be willing to let her go.

"What have you been talking with her about?" Berner asked from across the room.

I cleared my throat. "I know about their body systems," I told him.

"Good. Tell me."

Chapter 4

ξ

The Attack on the Hive

My days became very routine. I would wake up with the other Remnants and participate in the various exercises, martial arts sparring, and weapons training. Breakfast was a porridge, which we took from food vendors in the main square.

But I learned many things about the colony. Everyone had specific jobs to do. Construction workers reinforced the underground tunnels and living quarters continually.

There were food sellers who had networks that gathered food from different places above ground—but I also learned the colony could grow rice and beans, and so those comprised most of the food we ate.

The tailors made and mended clothing. Sanitation workers kept the water flowing and the sewers draining. The Remnants were security guards and made sure everyone followed the rules.

As Mert and Sashim had told me, there was a contingent of the population who didn't contribute. They were called the Dim, and consisted of nucksa and heifers who had been rescued but couldn't integrate properly into the colony society. Their brains could not understand social rules or normal expectations for behavior. Clearly, the abuse in the corrals had distorted their thinking—they didn't even have any notion of consent. The Dim spent most of their time fucking. Some colony members would even go down to the Dim's quarters and join in, when their biology called for it. Sometimes they were called upon to be soldiers, if the colony was attacked.

Mert and Sashim were often called back to the surface to guard. So I saw very little of them. I was designated as a teacher, so I stayed below, spending most of my time teaching Queen and several others how to read the Cabras's language. She wanted me to teach her how to understand their spoken words, but I told her human vocal cords could not make the alien language sounds.

At Queen's direction, our language classes started to happen with Ki'ichpanil as well. With me acting as an interpreter, I would have Ki'ichpanil say a word and then I would give a corresponding word Queen would understand. Ki'ichpanil was sometimes cooperative, but other times I was forced to manipulate words out of her. And even other times Ki'ichpanil would sulk in depression and not respond at all. So progress was painfully slow. Never mind the fact that it took me years as a pet to learn to understand.

Queen had other duties as leader of the colony, and so for most of the day, I was free to explore. I found an extensive collection of books in the colony's library. After I found a book that taught me how to read, and with a little help from Berner, I caught on quickly and was soon reading many of the works found in the library.

My favorite was one called *Origins of the Species*. Another book I found was called *War of the Worlds*. This one intrigued me because it was written before the Minotaur aliens had colonized our world, but it told a story about our world being conquered by an alien species. The aliens in the story had superior technology as well.

Queen let me do pretty much anything I wanted. But she had assigned Jenga to be my personal guard. At first, he wasn't interested in the books. In fact, he had never learned to read, and it took him longer to catch on. But he did like to share thoughts that he had. He was a deep thinker and asked questions we couldn't answer.

He also agreed to teach me the art of knife fighting, and so I spent hours in the Remnants' training gym, learning the various techniques. He was impressed by how quickly I adapted to the skill. He also taught me to fire a handgun. But the noise hurt my ears and the smell of smoke tickled my nostrils.

His dark hair, bushy eyebrows, stern face—which had a scar on the left cheek—and height made him look very intimidating. But his tone was always gentle and patient. I found it difficult to marry the two aspects of his nature.

Whenever Jenga was called away, Queen made sure Sashim was with me. I liked spending time with Sashim.

Seasons passed and I lost track because I spent all my time underground. It was one such time with Sashim that I learned the extent of the warring human colonies.

"Queen told me to stay with you today," she said. She always seemed so serious.

"Where's Jenga today?" I asked.

"I'm not sure," she replied. "Queen wanted him to check out some reports she received about disturbances on our southern borders."

"Disturbances?"

"Well, you know, other colonies attack each other. We have gone almost a year since our last skirmish."

"Is that a long time?"

"Yes," she said. "But it is nearing the end of the autumn season, and many other colonies are beginning to forage, kill, and steal for food to survive the winter. Sometimes we attack each other for things of value too."

"How many other colonies exist?"

"There are three that are a day's travel from us in each direction. That doesn't count the smaller colonies that are nomadic and hide wherever they are able."

"Are the other colonies as big as ours?"

"The other three I mentioned are. Because of Queen's leadership, we have excellent resources and supply systems. She always makes sure we have enough dried food stored for the winter."

"How long has Queen been leader?"

"She was elected into her role about ten years ago."

"She seems like a good leader, but could anyone replace her?"

Sashim eyed me quizzically. "Ambitions of leadership?" she asked.

I blushed. "No, absolutely not. I'm just curious. I mean, Queen can be abrasive and aloof, but overall, the colony seems to run smoothly."

"More or less," Sashim agreed. "If someone was unhappy with her leadership, they could issue a challenge during a meeting. As you know, we have them monthly. Immediately, upon a challenge, there is a vote. If the vote goes against Queen, then the challenger assumes the role of leader."

"That seems like you could have leadership turn over monthly."

"That's how it used to be. There are very few challenges now."

"How could anything be accomplished?"

"It couldn't, which is why people only challenge now during big disagreements, and Queen still wins though. People are more inclined to support the one they know. Someone else could really shake things up, and it could be hugely detrimental to our colony's survival. We need to make sure our leader has the time and support to make decisions and plan a course for our future. The colony almost starved to death in its first winter. Queen's great-grandmother was the one who eventually took the role and made things happen. Queen's family has been leading us now for two generations."

"Where are the other colonies?"

"Come with me," she announced. "I'll show you."

I followed her out of the Remnants' quarters and she took me to the tunnel that led to Queen's area.

As soon as we entered, I noticed a shift in the decorative look of the colony. Queen's quarters were not furnished with bunks like other places. Pictures hung on the walls.

"Art?" I asked. I had seen some pictures in books from the library. But I was surprised that they had real art on the walls.

"Beautiful paintings," Sashim said. "The humans from before made them."

"How did the humans from before create them?"

Sashim shrugged. "I have no idea. But they also made practical things."

She led me down one of six tunnels that diverged from the meeting room.

"This is our museum room," she said.

"It isn't guarded," I stated.

"It doesn't need to be. Everyone is allowed to walk through here. It is all we have left of history."

"Isn't Queen afraid people will steal it for themselves?"

"There is some theft. But we share everything, so it's difficult to call it stealing. The only possessions that people are allowed to claim as their own are the tools of their trade—and you will find most people are willing to share even those."

My hand went unconsciously to the knife at my belt and the blowgun along my back. These were mine. I would never give them up.

"How have you learned to live like this?" I was truly stumped. In the corrals, we fought for everything. We even had felt ownership over the food if we got to the trough first.

Sashim's tone got quieter. "One of the reasons our colony split from the previous tribe two generations ago. There, people fought for possessions. There were even cases of murder, all because someone wanted another colony member's possession.

"Queen's great-grandmother, Nakota, decided that their tribe would not have possessions, aside from tools needed for one to do their trade. Everyone who came with her agreed to that rule."

"But you don't share with other tribes?"

"No, we protect to the death our food, our way of life, and our people."

Sashim went to a globe and brought it over to me. "This is a map of our planet," she explained. She pointed to a place near the middle to top part of the globe. "This is where our colony is located. We call ourselves Nakota."

"What's that?" I pointed to a large black dot drawn on the globe; it was located near the colony. Another twenty or so black dots encircled the globe.

"Those are the alien cities we know about on the surface of our world."

"How do you know about the other ones?"

"Um." Sashim paused. "We can listen to and communicate

with other humans."

"I thought you fought each other." My new world was difficult to comprehend. Humans attacking each other for food, yet somehow connected enough to share information.

"There are millions of humans around the world," she said. "Many—most—live on the Cabras farms. But there are colonies like ours all over the planet. And though we fight each other for food, we also share information about the movement of Cabras."

"There are free people everywhere? Why don't we fight the aliens?"

"We tried, at first." She picked up a book called *The Real Minotaur* and flipped it open. "When they arrived, their machine of war immediately took out most of our world's weapons, including nuclear warheads. Then, using their Reaper-bots, they wiped out our armies. We are the ones that launched any remaining missiles, which is why there are large scorched areas, like the one above us."

"But surely, humans have tried to kill the Cabras?" I said it as a statement, but meant it as a question.

"We've never been able to kill a Cabras, not for hundreds of years. We can't get close to them."

"But I paralyzed them so easily. I'm surprised no one figured that much out." How could these humans be so stupid? I wondered.

"I can't explain it to you," Sashim admitted. "It's why you are so special."

"But I found this blowgun, so someone else must have figured it out."

"Maybe," she replied. "But the knowledge was never passed along. And no other human seems able to get close enough to use weapons. We never have a chance."

A loud siren went off, and the lights dimmed.

"What's going on?" I asked.

"We are under attack. Come on!" Sashim ordered. "Stay with me; I'll keep you safe. Don't let yourself get captured."

"Why would anyone want to capture me?"

"You are a wealth of information. If news got out that we have someone who understands the alien's language, they'd want to take you."

I followed her out of the room. My hand was on the knife at my belt. "But if they want me, and news about my being here got out, they might want the Cabras that taught me the language."

Sashim looked back at me. She understood immediately. "We need to protect Ki'ichpanil. No one else can have her."

The common cavern was a mass of chaos. I couldn't tell who was fighting who, or how they could tell each other apart.

"What do I do?" I asked.

"You fight anyone who attacks you."

We pushed through the throng. At first, people left us alone, content to let us go our way. Once we made it to the science quarters, the chaos lightened up and we easily reached Berner and Ki'ichpanil. There were a few other Remnants who had been posted there, waiting.

Sashim and I joined them.

Ten men and women stormed into the room.

"Dive behind cover," Sashim ordered, shoving me behind a table.

The attackers started firing their guns. I remembered how bullets were a commodity and rarely used. But this attack was evidently an exception.

The Remnants opened return fire. Bullets ricocheted off the walls. But miraculously no one was struck. Eventually, they all emptied their clips and the attackers pulled out knives and stormed farther into the room.

A dark-haired girl confronted me. She held a long knife in her hand. She had the same fighting style as me, our blades waving slightly like shields in front of our bodies.

But she suddenly attacked with ferocity. Because I had trained so much with Jenga, I was able to block and fight back, allowing myself to make small cuts wherever I could, then dodging backward.

Her blade continually found the soft places on the back of my biceps and forearms. But each time she struck, I was able to get an effective counterstrike in, slicing at her sides, arms, and legs.

Thankfully, Jenga had also taught me to use my whole body in a knife fight, kicking, punching, and stabbing.

The dark-haired enemy made a fatal mistake and overextended her reach, giving me an opportunity to jab my blade into her side.

Her mouth opened and her eyes blinked rapidly as her blood flowed over my hand. I jabbed harder and farther into her flesh. Tears sprung to her eyes, and then suddenly, I saw her pupils dilate and she went limp in my arms. I swear I felt her spirit leaving her body. I dropped her to the floor.

I couldn't take full stock of the situation in the room; my eyes were blurry, and my brain was in a fog. A wave of nausea washed over me. The Remnants were losing.

Sashim made her way to my side. "We have to flee! Run for your life! There are too many of them! Come on!" Sashim ordered, pulling at my arm.

I reluctantly followed her. Berner was standing next to the cage, and we reached him in a moment. The Remnants held back the attackers long enough for the three of us to escape through a back entrance, into the tunnels, leaving Ki'ichpanil to the attackers. The dead woman's blood felt sticky between my fingers and the nausea returned.

Chapter 5

ξ

The Counterattack

After the sounds of fighting diminished, Sashim, Berner, and I returned to the science wing. It had been utterly destroyed. The bodies of our fellow Remnants lay scattered on the floor, and the cage that had held Ki'ichpanil was damaged, the door hanging by busted hinges. Old tech lay shattered from bullets penetrating it, tables were upturned, and there was so much glass on the floor. I wasn't even sure where it all came from.

"How did they manage to move her?" Sashim asked. "She's stronger than them."

Berner walked to a drawer at the back of the room and opened it. He gave an audible sigh of relief and held up the four golden rings. "They didn't get these. I assume our Cabras is no threat without them. She has become much weakened without them."

I barely heard what they were saying as I walked over to the body of the woman I had killed. She had dark hair and a skinny frame, much like mine. Her brown eyes were open and glossy. I stood there, staring at her body. I didn't feel victorious. I felt empty and despondent. I had taken something precious, and this feeling I had was new.

I lowered myself to one knee and picked up her knife. It had some of my dried blood on the blade.

"Why?" I asked. "Why are humans killing each other? I don't

understand. This is such a fucking waste."

We heard footsteps and voices coming up the tunnel. I held my dark-haired enemy's knife, ready to fight.

Jenga entered the room first. His gaze found me. "Thank god you're okay," he said.

Queen was right behind him. "Fuck, they got the Cabras. We've got to get her back. We counterstrike right now. Gather all the Remnants you can! Also, get the nucksa to head the charge," she ordered one of her guards. He left immediately.

"I'm going too," I declared.

Jenga approached me and held up my arm, examining my wounds. "You need to get patched up," he said.

"I'm fucking fine!" I retorted. "I want to go too!"

"No way," Queen said. "You are far too valuable to lose in battle."

Jenga glanced back at Queen. "She should come." His tone was sincere yet firm. "She just wants to feel like she is contributing." He spoke for me, and I gave him a glare.

Queen mulled his comment over, her facial features contemplative, not angry for Jenga challenging her.

"Fine, but get her a bulletproof vest."

Another guard disappeared down the tunnel. Jenga came over to me and pulled a handgun out of the holster at his hip. He pulled back on the top, and I heard a click as a cartridge slid into place.

"Here."

I nodded as he gave me the handgun. It was cool in my hand and heavy.

"Good. But you must stay with me the whole time." His tone was brusque.

I nodded again as I gripped the handle.

We exited the science wing. Already a hundred people had gathered—fifty Remnants and fifty nucksa. The Remnants held real weapons, knives and guns, whereas the nucksa held sticks and bats.

"How does this work?" I asked Jenga.

"We are going to strike the other tribe before they reach the safety of their colony."

"But they've got to be miles ahead of us."

"We have a train."

My face twisted in confusion. "A train?"

"It's our version of a transport. Except ours doesn't hover like the Cabras; ours travels on rails."

"Why didn't the other tribe use it?"

My gaze met Jenga's eyes. I loved Jenga's eyes, but they seemed hard right now. "The other tribe call themselves the Stoney People. And they didn't take the train because they don't know about it."

"I don't understand."

"Deep underneath our colony, there is a set of ancient tracks. We found them long ago. We only recently learned how to make the trains operate. They travel all over, underground. We can get ahead of the Stoney People."

I nodded and followed Jenga to the head of the army.

"What do the nucksa do?" I asked him.

"They are the first assault. They keep the enemy busy, so we can get in and accomplish our mission. We must get your Ki'ichpanil back."

"Will they be hurt?"

Jenga didn't reply right away. "Many of them will be killed."

That felt wrong. But I finally felt like I was beginning to understand the reality that free humans lived with. They were like animals hiding and just hoping to survive. It was a world of kill or be killed; I wasn't sure I could be a part of it.

"Come on," Jenga ordered. His tone was loud and official. "To the train!" he hollered. "Take it all!"

"Take it all!" The army returned his cry, hollering loudly.

The train was shaped like a couple of boxes with windows. The windows were empty, and the army crawled through every opening.

"How do you power it?"

Jenga pulled me to the front of the first car. "Like this," he said. He pointed to a console holding a small key, which he turned to the "on" position. "It runs on an electrical current. We couldn't make it run before because we couldn't get a strong enough current. But Berner saved us; he figured it out."

Jenga pointed to wires along the ceiling of the tunnel we faced. "Using solar-powered batteries from the surface, we can power the train."

"So, how often have you used it?"

"We've only done some trial runs. But this is the first time we've used it to counterstrike."

The humming intensified as Jenga pushed a lever forward and the train started to move. It jolted a couple of times, and I staggered to catch my balance.

It took a minute or so for the train to pick up speed. I felt the wind press against my chest as I stared into the black tunnel in front of us.

"How far?" I hollered above the wind.

"Far enough to get ahead of them," he yelled back. "There is a place just up here where we will stop and gain access to the tunnel the attackers used. With any luck, we will be ahead of them."

The tunnel suddenly widened into a large platform, and Jenga pulled back on the lever, slowing the train to a stop. The nucksa jumped off the train first, before it had even come to a stop.

Like wild men, they ran up a set of stairs. The Remnants, including Jenga and I, followed them. At the top of the stairs there was a pair of sealed metal doors. The nucksa crashed into them. After only a few moments of pounding, they broke through into another tunnel.

They turned right, and I thought we were heading back toward our hive.

"You're sure we are ahead of them?" I asked.

Jenga nodded.

In response, I heard yells as our nucksa reached the Stoney People tribe. They were caught entirely by surprise.

The fighting created a blockage, and we couldn't move forward.

"There are too many people," I yelled over the din.

"Come on," Jenga said, his tone determined. "We're getting to the Cabras."

He pushed through the fighting. My knife was in my hands, ready should I need to defend myself. I could feel the handgun against the small of my back.

Jenga crashed through, firing his weapon; many nucksa from the other tribe fell to the ground as he cleared the path. He didn't show any fear. His stoic expression suggested that he didn't even care he was killing other humans.

It seemed an unwritten rule of warfare: our nucksa fought the other tribe's nucksa, and warriors fought other warriors.

Jenga and I, along with a dozen other Remnants, pushed to the back of the raging battle until I saw Ki'ichpanil. She was surrounded by twenty of the enemy. They had wrapped her in ropes and were dragging her through the tunnel. There was a glimmer of light in her eyes, like she knew something. She was no longer afraid. I looked around. Were we still below ground or inside a collapsed subway station above ground? But the thought disappeared as we rushed forward.

The first person I came upon was a man a few years older than me. He aimed a gun at my chest. I jumped aside, falling to the floor. As I dove, I pulled the gun Jenga had given me from the back of my belt. I fired, but the bullet flew wildly off target.

He pulled his own trigger at the same time. I heard the bang and felt the breath knocked out of me. Pain seared into my chest; had the bullet gone right through the bulletproof vest Queen had given me? He pulled the trigger on his gun again, but he must have used up his ammunition, because the gun only clicked.

Jumping to my feet, I fired again and again; this time, my bullets found their target and he dropped to the ground. It was easier to kill from a distance, I realized. The distance diminished my sense of loss and guilt at taking the man's life. I felt detached from it.

The wind returned to my lungs, and I looked down at my chest. There was no blood. I stuck my hand in behind the vest to feel if the bullet had gone through. There was no wound, but my nerves were definitely sensitive to the touch and I cringed.

The battle ended quickly because the Stoney People tribe had used all their ammunition in their attack, not considering that we would be able to counterattack them so quickly. Since we had rearmed, we killed most of them while a few of the rest fled.

Ki'ichpanil, still trussed up, kept glancing up at me. I couldn't communicate with her without the tablet.

Jenga arrived by my side with several nucksa who had survived.

"Are you okay?" he asked. "I wasn't able to get to your side, but I saw the guy fire his gun."

I nodded weakly. "It's a good thing I was wearing this." I wrapped my knuckles on the vest.

He smiled. His face relaxed. "I'm glad you're safe," he said. "Good shot, by the way," he added.

"Thanks," I mumbled shyly. I could feel my cheeks turning warm. I turned my head so he wouldn't notice.

But he was already directing the nucksa with him. "Pick the Cabras up and bring her to the train," he ordered.

I walked quietly behind Ki'ichpanil, who was being carried down the tunnel by five nucksa. Was she glad to be back with us?

The train ran in reverse, and we were silent as we returned. We had won the attack and recovered everything taken from the Remnants. But I didn't feel right. It was so easy to kill other humans. I didn't like it. But the other tribe was so intent on killing us; what choice did we have? What choice did I have?

"Is it always like this?" I asked suddenly. "Do we ever get to feel safe?"

"Yes, it's always like this," Jenga replied. His tone was dull. "No one is ever safe."

I glanced back at Ki'ichpanil. She didn't look nearly as frightened as she had before. Suddenly, I thought of a terrifying reason for her lack of fear. Had she been able to communicate with another Cabras, telepathically?

Part 4

The Existence

Chapter 1

ξ

The Nucksa

The central cavern of our hive was strangely quiet. People were still milling around, but they spoke in hushed tones. Upon returning to our tribe, Jenga took Ki'ichpanil back to the science wing. I just sat down on a bench. A feeling of sadness came over me at the realization I had taken the lives of two humans.

I watched as the Dim returned to their tunnel and disappeared into its darkness. Jenga saw them as fodder for the machine of war, and they seemed content to follow orders, even to their deaths. They had lost the ability to think for themselves.

My thoughts turned to Jenga. He had been a bullaman before he was rescued. He was strong and stern, but he had a softer side. I only knew a little about his history. He didn't like to open up too much about it. But he had been a bullaman in a white-domed farm. However, he told me most bullamans quickly took the role seriously and inseminated as many heifers as they could; Jenga did not.

Jenga was too passive. At least, that was what he said. He would only inseminate heifers who came to him and offered themselves, which quite a few did. However, he didn't inseminate enough heifers to make the Overseers happy, so they sold him to another farm. He's probably lucky he wasn't turned into a nucksa.

I felt the tingling in my stomach again, thinking about Jenga, and I tried to push his image from my mind.

My feet took me toward the Dim's tunnel; it was the only place in our hive I hadn't visited yet. Sashim had warned me not to go down there, even though I had seen her go there. I wasn't sure why.

Nucksa and heifers, heifers and heifers, and nucksa and nucksa formed couple groups along the walls. At times, three of them all grouped together, kissing each other and fondling each other's body parts.

I entered their room, affectionally called the bordello. It wasn't decorated nicely, like the rest of the hive, though they had pillows for lounging on. There had to be thousands of heifers and nucksa in the room. Some arrived from doors encircling the main hall.

"Hello," a voice said behind me. I turned abruptly to find myself face-to-face with a nucksa. He was around my age—maybe a couple of years younger, eighteen or even seventeen. He stood very close to me, and I could feel his breath on my face as I tried to take a step backward. He wasn't wearing a shirt, and his hairless skin was white and pasty. His blond hair and overly red lips formed a shocking contrast.

He stepped with me, and I felt apprehension pressing on my heart as it palpitated rapidly. "Excuse me," I said. I tried to push past him, back toward the exit.

"Where are you going?" His voice was oddly calm, like he was intoxicated. "Stay for a puff of weed," he said. He pulled out a joint from a pocket on his loose-fitting slacks.

"No thanks." I once again tried to push by.

His hand came up and restrained me, resting on my hip. His grip was firm, and even though I didn't want to hurt him, I was ready to defend myself.

"It'll relax you," the blond nucksa said.

He kept his hand firmly on my waist. Then he pulled me into him. I pressed my hands on his chest, resisting him.

"Come on now," he said with an intoxicated whisper. "Why else would you have come down here?"

We were beginning to draw the attention of others in the room, and a heifer came up behind him. Like me, she was dark-haired with sad blue eyes; she was also shirtless. Her finger trailed along the nucksa's shoulders and mine until she stood behind me. I glanced back at her as her arms surrounded my waist and I felt her breasts pressed hard into my back.

"You should take this off," she whispered into my ear, her hands pulling at the fabric of my leather vest.

"No," I said more forcefully. I tried to push the nucksa's hands off my hips, but he held me tight and started to gyrate his hips against mine as the heifer behind me did the same.

A feeling of anxiety rose in my chest, and I could feel my breaths coming in shorter gasps. My two oppressors took this as a sign to press against me harder.

The nucksa's hands moved to my ass, and the touch sent shivers up my spine, even though I was repulsed by it. The heifer behind me slid her hands under my hands and grasped one of my breasts. I could feel the palm of her hand pressed firmly against my nipple, and I tried to rebuke it from responding, but it instantly hardened.

"Get off me," I said in a panic. But their hands kept exploring my body, touching me everywhere. "Get off," I practically screamed.

Unfortunately, my resistance drew the attention of another nucksa, who joined in, running his hands over my skin.

As I tried to fight them, the blond nucksa found the zipper on my leather vest and pulled it down in a fluid motion, exposing my breasts. Her hands found my nipples again and she played with them between her fingers. My rose between my legs became moist. My body was responding to the touches without my permission.

I felt hands brushing my thigh, around the hem of my leather skirt, hands pulling at the hem, trying to lift it.

"No! No!" I shouted. "Get off me! No, you can't have it. You can't have it!" I sobbed; my voice was panicked.

I felt utterly powerless to stop the assault on my body; it was like I was a heifer back in the corral, with a bullaman forcing himself to inseminate me.

I felt the power in my legs giving way, and I was about to collapse.

"Back the fuck up!" a strong voice ordered.

The hands let go of me and I fell to the floor, exhausted from the assault. Jenga was standing there with a pistol pointed at the head of the blond-haired nucksa.

"Are you all right?" he asked, not taking his eyes off the nucksa.

I nodded weakly, quickly standing and zipping up the vest, covering myself again. I felt weak and relaxed at the same time.

"What are you doing down here?" he asked.

"I was just curious. Sashim comes down here sometimes. But I didn't really think about the fact that the dim have been so brainwashed by the corrals, that they wouldn't think about consent."

"We all have needs." He smiled, holstering his gun. The two nucksa and the heifer had backed off and were now making out with each other.

"Is that why you're here?" I asked.

"No," he replied. "One of the Remnants saw you head down the tunnel. I came to find you right away."

"Thank you," I whispered. He placed a firm hand on my shoulder and walked with me back out of the nucksa and heifer area.

"So, Sashim likes to have sex with other people?"

"Sure," Jenga replied. "Some people like to have it often and with lots of different people. Sashim, for example, is bi and will have sex with both nucksa and heifers. Most of the people down there are bi."

"What are the other kinds of people?" I asked, intrigued. My thoughts returned to the corrals, and specifically Seffie. Maybe I was bi as well. I enjoyed the times with Seffie.

"Some other people," Jenga replied, "prefer to be in monogamous relationships."

"What does that mean?"

"Only one sexual partner at a time, like me. That's why I wasn't a very good bullaman."

"Oh," I said quietly. I wondered if he was now in a monogamous relationship.

"I like to feel connected with the person I am having sex with. Sure, sex feels great, but it feels so much better when I know the person has feelings for me and I have feelings for them."

This information felt so new and so foreign. "Sorry, I don't understand what you mean by feelings. I mean, I know what feelings are: anger, fear, happiness. But how does that relate to sex? Isn't sex just a physical act?"

"I don't think so," Jenga said, smiling.

We reached our hive's main hub, and he took me to a food stall, where we sat down on a bench.

"Well, when I have feelings for someone, I care about what happens to them. I think about them. I think about them so much; I look for them everywhere I am. Sometimes I will see another person, and all it does is remind me of the one I have feelings for. We call them feels, but I think it's just a happy feeling in my heart when they are around. And when I have sex with them, that feeling is exponentiated."

I lowered my gaze. "Are you in a monogamous relationship now?" I asked quietly.

"No." He smiled. But his smile was melancholy.

"Were you ever?"

He nodded. "I had feelings for a heifer when I was a bullaman. We would spend every moment together, and I gave her all my attention. The Overseers tried to separate us, but I went on a rampage and started destroying the corral they placed me in."

"What happened?"

"They killed her. Right in front of me."

"What?" I was shocked. "Why did they kill her and not you?"

He sneered. "Bullaman are worth a lot. The Overseers don't like to see an investment gone to waste, so they sold me."

"I'm sorry," I said.

"It's in the past," he said. "Look, I have a meeting with Queen, so I need to leave now. Will you be okay?"

I nodded.

"Okay, just don't go back down that tunnel—unless, of course, you want to participate in an orgy."

Time passed quickly. I spent my time, as always, teaching Queen and the others how to understand the alien's language.

Ki'ichpanil had become even more withdrawn and sullen. Berner was focused on the gold rings and had me ask her many questions, but she refused to answer any of them. I was pretty sure she had no idea how they worked.

Everywhere I went, I looked for Jenga. Whenever there was a meeting and Queen addressed the colony, I watched him standing next to her and wished I could go and stand with him.

When he brought Queen to the small room we used for her instruction, I felt happiness at seeing him. And my heart soared even higher when I would catch him looking at me too. We would find every moment we could just to be in each other's presence.

About a week after the attack on the colony, I was sitting by the food stall in the main hub when I saw Jenga walking through the crowd. He hadn't noticed me yet. I watched him as his gaze darted around the room like he was looking for someone. Then his gaze rested on me, and I could see a palpable change in demeanor; he relaxed and smiled. I waved at him.

I gulped as I realized I was feeling the feels for Jenga. I wanted to be in a relationship with him.

He motioned to me to follow him. I stood and strode to his side. "I'm so happy to see you," I whispered. His hand reached over and he clasped my hand. Immediately a jolt of pleasure ran through my whole body and I found myself smiling.

A few moments later, in a deserted tunnel, we stopped and faced each other.

He breathed out quietly.

"What?" I asked, suddenly hesitant.

"I have feelings for you," he replied quickly. "I think about you all the time. When I'm working, I want to be with you. When I see you, my heart leaps and I feel myself having tunnel vision. I just want to be with you."

I didn't let him keep talking. I lifted my hands and pulled his lips to mine to kiss him.

Chapter 2

ξ

Bullfighting

The library was just a small room, but books lined the walls from floor to ceiling. Berner had told me that the books were scavenged from ruins.

I liked to sit on the floor in the room and read books. There was no other furniture, but I was comfortable enough with my back against the shelf. As I read, the smell of the old paper wafted into my nostrils.

I was in the midst of a book when Berner entered the room. He always shuffled when he walked. I barely glanced up at him.

He also spent a lot of time in the library. He placed a thick leather-bound book on the shelf and pulled a paperback with a white cover from next to it. Tucking it under his arm, he glanced over at me.

"What are you reading?" he asked.

I flipped the book closed, but left my finger as a marker for the page I was on. "It's called *Death in the Afternoon* by an author named Ernest Hemmingway."

"I've read it," Berner remarked. "Hemmingway seems to be okay with bullfighting as an event. He wrote something about things being morally right if when after watching an event you feel fine."

I shook my head. "I found it because of the title. But I've learned interesting things about human culture from before the

Minotaurs arrived."

"What specifically?" Berner asked.

"Humans from before weren't any better than the aliens are now. We killed animals for sport."

Berner shook his head. "But they were animals. I don't understand your revulsion."

I blinked at him. "You know that the Minotaurs think we are animals. To them we are lesser beings."

He nodded contemplatively.

"But bullfighting is even more cruel." I flipped back a few pages. "Listen to this at the beginning of chapter two: 'The bullfight is not a sport...it is not an equal contest or an attempt at an equal contest between a bull and a man. Rather it is a tragedy; the death of the bull...' It is set up to kill the bull for the entertainment of the crowd." I paused.

"I suppose, then, it is a moral question," Berner mused. "I'm not a philosopher, but a scientist. I can agree that killing anything for sport is morally reprehensible. However, is killing to eat also such?"

"It is disgusting that the Cabras eat humans for food," I said. "Just because the aliens consider themselves superior beings, with superior technology, and with language we cannot understand, doesn't make our flesh a justifiable food source."

Jenga entered the library, interrupting our conversation. "Hey," he said. "I have a few minutes. I was just looking for you."

"Do you think it is okay that the Cabras eat human flesh?" I asked.

He was startled by the abruptness of my question. "Ah, no," he said. He glanced at Berner.

"We're no better than the Cabras," I said. I only had a basic sense and understanding about philosophy and morality. But in my heart, I knew that there are things that are right, and things that are wrong.

"Anyway," Berner said, changing his tone. He dug into his pocket. "I did come here hoping to find you for another reason." He pulled out one of the gold rings.

Standing up, I took one of the rings into my hands and felt the smoothness of the metal.

"I need you to come speak to Ki'ichpanil about the rings," he said.

"Why?" I asked.

"I want to see if there is a way for us to use the technology."

Jenga glanced up. "I only have a few minutes before Queen will want me back."

I nodded at Berner. "I'll find you after," I said, and handed the gold ring back to him.

Berner nodded and left the library. Jenga came over and clasped my hand with our fingers interlocking. "I just needed to spend some time with you," he said.

Since our first kiss, we had spent every moment we could find together. We would often sneak into different abandoned tunnels to kiss. I loved kissing him. It stirred my passion as our lips touched and he held me close.

"We can stay here, if you want. Tell me about what you are reading today," he said.

I smiled mischievously. I had other ideas what I wanted to do with him.

Leaving the library, I led him to one of our favorite tunnels. It was past the science area and led to an exit from the colony a dozen miles away. No one used it.

His hand felt warm in mine. I shifted my blowgun, satchel, and knife as we walked. “What do you like about me?” I asked him.

“Your eyes,” he said. “There is fire in them, like nothing can contain you, and I just want to be a part of that passion. I want to be consumed by your spirit. It’s like you are the freest person in the world, and when I am with you, I also feel that spirit of freedom.”

I smiled at his awkward stumbling over words.

“It is difficult to explain,” he admitted. “You’re very attractive too.”

I rested my head against his shoulder as we walked. “I find you attractive too,” I said. In that moment I should have said more. I should have told him that when I was with him, I felt like a more complete version of myself; like we were destined to be together. But I didn’t. Instead, I just allowed myself to be content in his presence. Hoping and dreaming that it would last forever.

As soon as we were in the deserted tunnel, we stopped and faced each other. The smell of dirt was everywhere. But it didn’t matter. I rested my hands on Jenga’s forearms. The muscle there was firm. He in turn placed his hands on my sides, just above my hips, and a good thrill ran through my body.

Standing up on my tiptoes, I turned my face to his.

Chapter 3

ξ

The Lover

Jenga's mouth pressed hard against my lips, and I could taste the sweetness of his breath. The smell of his body titillated my senses as his hand came up and rested on my breast. I felt a tingling sensation run through every nerve of my body, and my nipple hardened under his touch.

Slowly, we knelt on the floor. The deserted tunnel, everyone else, the colony, and even the memory of the corrals disappeared, and all I could think about was this moment. We unbuckled our belts and let our weapons drop to the floor. I unslung my blowgun and satchel.

I lifted my hand to his face and pulled his mouth closer, wanting to feel every inch of his kiss as we lay beside each other. The floor was cool against my legs, but I ignored it.

His mouth closed slightly, and I let my lips linger on his. His hand left my breast and moved to the zipper on my leather vest. Cautiously, he pulled the vest open and slid it just past my shoulders, exposing my breasts. He leaned down and gently ran his tongue around my areola. Then he closed his mouth over my entire nipple and sucked on it gently. Bolts of electric pleasure pulsated through my body.

I took his hand and brought it down to my side, close to the hem of my leather skirt. His hand firmly cupped my ass, and a sensation of desire ran up my spine again. He continued to massage my ass and lower back as he brought his mouth back to my nipple.

With my eyelids fluttering, I tried to watch his face as he teased my nipple. I wanted more of him touching me. I wanted him to touch more of me. I pushed the vision of the bullaman inseminating Seffie out of my mind and instead thought of Deliav. She had wanted the bullaman to touch her rose.

As I arched my body in response to Jenga's touch and tongue, I reached and took his hand. Spreading my legs, I placed his hand on the area above my rose. I desperately wanted him to touch me, to make this feeling in my soul come alive. It was a fire of passion burning in my heart, and I wanted it to burst out.

His mouth alternated between my nipple and mouth.

His hands explored all parts of my body, and I found myself involuntarily spreading my legs in response to him. The feeling was euphoric, vastly different from when the nucksa had touched me.

Kneeling, he moved between my legs and stripped off my vest and skirt. I was fully naked in front of him, and he lowered his face to my rose. I felt hesitant at first, but I trusted him, and I let him place his tongue on my rose. The feeling was instant as tremors ran the gamut through my body. His tongue moved along all parts of my rose, and he firmly pressed my knees to my chest.

One of his hands cupped my ass, and I felt him insert a finger into my rose. My breath caught in my throat; I moaned, the pleasure cascading over me. His tongue licked the top of my rose.

Unconsciously, I let out a sigh as I rested my hands on the back of his head, pulling him closer to my body. I breathed heavily, and I felt momentarily light-headed as Jenga sat up and rubbed the tip of my rose more vigorously. I pulled him up to me and kissed him passionately. A feeling of imminent release built within me, within my rose, within my soul. I wanted him to massage faster, but he pulled back, and again his mouth pressed against mine in a hard kiss, his tongue playing with mine.

Then I rolled him onto his back and sat on top of him. He lay back as I rolled his black T-shirt over his shoulders, exposing his bare chest. He had finely chiseled features, and sparse hair covered his pecs and trailed thinly down to his waist. I unbuttoned his pants.

He rested his arms behind his head as his dark eyes watched me. I knew he wanted me, but he wouldn't force me; he let me take control.

As I slid his pants down, I saw his bullaman, but I didn't want to call it that; that term was too negative. I saw his cock. It was already hard, and as I took his pants past his feet, I saw it twitch. It was about twice as long as the width of my hand, and I wondered if it would hurt. I remembered watching Seffie's face as the bullaman shoved inside of her. She looked in pain. But this felt different; what Jenga and I were doing was passionate, not violent.

Shoving the thought out of my head, I brought my hand up to his cock and held it. The skin was soft, and I could practically feel his soul vibrating, pulsating, in it. I stroked my hand along the entire shaft, and his body responded to my touch. His back arched slightly and his lips pursed with each stroke of my hand.

Straddling his leg, I was conscious of my wet rose touching his skin, and I moved my hips in sync as I stroked his cock. Each thrust of my hips reinvigorated the desire I felt for him. Once again, the sensation of imminent release built within me.

I wanted to taste him, just as he had tasted me. I lowered my mouth to his erect shaft. At first, I just let my lips and tongue play with the head while my hand gently massaged him. A groan slipped past his lips as mine encircled his swollen cock. I glanced up with my eyes; his were closed.

Unconsciously, his hips pressed up, pushing his cock farther into my mouth. I liked the taste of it. I moved my mouth and hands faster and felt his body responding. His hand rested gently on the back of my head, and he pushed my hair out of his line of sight so he could watch my mouth and tongue on his cock.

I slid my mouth over the top of his cock and massaged it with my hand. He pulled me up to his mouth, and again, we kissed passionately. My rose cried out for more. I wanted him inside of me.

I straddled him, and I felt his hard cock between my legs, just resting there. I moved my hips, allowing my rose to caress his entire shaft.

His arms came up behind me and he rolled me over onto my back. My feet were in the air, with my knees pressed firmly to my sides. I wanted him to be inside me. I reached my hands down, grasped his erection, and directed it toward my rose.

The tip of his cock pressed against my flower, and I sucked in a breath.

An alarm sounded. I looked up at Jenga and saw disappointment on his face.

"What is it?" I asked him, panting.

"It is an alert. We are going to attack a transport."

"Do you have to go?"

"Yes," he replied solemnly.

"But I need you," I whispered into his ear.

"We have to stop; people might be coming down this tunnel any moment." He lay back down beside me. "I want to share myself with you too," he said. "But we only have a few minutes. And I don't want to rush this. I'm sorry."

The disappointment washed over me like a turbulent wave,

but I stood and pulled my skirt and leather vest back over my shaking body. This pissed me off.

Even though we didn't finish our lovemaking, I was still hyperaware of where his hand had touched my skin, where his tongue had touched my rose and breast, and where his lips had pressed on my lips.

I reached up and tenderly touched my lips. That first kiss I would remember for the rest of my life. My anger subsided, but not my desire to feel his cock inside me.

Chapter 4

ξ

The Gold Rings' Power

"There you are!" Queen hissed as we approached. Queen was standing with the other Remnants. "We just received word that a transport is scheduled to come through the pass."

"They are transporting food," Jenga whispered into my ear. Jenga took his place next to Queen, but his vision stayed on me. I saw him adjust his pants, just over his groin, and I smiled.

"Wait!" a voice called out. It was Berner. "Queen, wait! This is important."

Berner was running out of the tunnel that led to the science wing.

"What is it, Berner?" she asked. "The transport won't wait for us. We need to be in position, on time!"

"I know, I know," he said quickly. "But I need Zee and Jenga."

Queen shook her head. "Jenga stays with me, but Zee can stay with you; we don't need her for this attack."

Berner shook his head. "Please, I need Jenga for this matter; it will take but a moment. I am sure they will be able to catch up before you reach the transport."

Queen was hesitant. "He better," she warned.

"Come with me," Berner said to Jenga and me.

What could be so important? I wondered. No one ever contradicted Queen.

"What's the trouble?" Jenga asked as we followed Berner into the science wing.

"There is no trouble," he replied mysteriously. But he refused to say more until we were in the lab.

Sitting on a table near Ki'ichpanil's cage were the golden rings. Ki'ichpanil was sullener than I had ever seen her before.

"I figured it out," Berner announced.

"What?" I asked.

"The rings. I know how they work. I needed to ask the alien some questions, but time is limited, now."

"Why did you need me for this?" Jenga asked.

Berner smiled knowingly. "I know the two of you have feelings for each other, and because of that, I would like you both to participate in a bit of an experiment."

"I'm listening," I said. I stood next to Jenga; it made me feel more confident.

"The rings are typically connected to tissue. As we know, we had to cut them off the aliens' hands. But we had no idea how the rings connected to their hands, or if they were actually part of their flesh. But if they were, the rings should have 'died' when severed from their host bodies."

"But the rings didn't," Jenga finished.

"That's right. The rings are technological, and this technology is connected to the alien bodies."

"We assumed all this," I said. I glanced at Jenga, his fingers tapping lightly against his crossed arms.

"Right, but I know how to connect them," Berner said.

"How?" I said.

"I placed the rings under a microscope."

I raised my eyebrows.

"I found tiny strings, as small as nerve endings in the human body. But then, I placed the ring on my finger and looked at it under the microscope."

"What happened?" I asked.

Berner beamed. "They came alive."

"What do you mean?"

"The tiny strings started to move about, searching my skin for a connection. But they couldn't find one."

"What were they searching for?"

Berner paused. "I hypothesize they are looking for nerve endings to connect to."

"How could you possibly attach nerve endings to the ring?" Jenga asked, and I nodded.

"That's why we need to conduct an experiment. I chose Zee because she already understands the alien language, and I have no idea what will happen if I successfully connect the ring to human tissue."

I raised an eyebrow again.

Berner clarified. "Since you can understand the language, if you hear them talking, you'll be able to understand what they are saying. The experiment I want to try is very dangerous. Your ability to understand them will help alleviate some, but not all, of that danger."

"But why me?" asked Jenga.

"Because I want to know if you and Zee will be able to communicate with each other telepathically, like we suspect the aliens do. We could learn all kinds of things about their civilization. We might be able to learn how to use the force field. If we learn that, we will be able to fight back."

I felt a bit apprehensive. We had no idea what would

transpire if I put on one of the rings. The one thing I knew was I never wanted to be a prisoner again. I sighed. "Okay, how does this work? I assume you know how to connect our nerves to the strings." I glanced over at Ki'ichpanil. She was watching us intently speaking about the rings.

Berner smiled knowingly again. "I won't have to. All I have to do is make an incision around your finger where you want the ring. After that, the ring will do the rest."

"Why will that work?" I asked.

"I think the ring will find the nerve endings and connect automatically."

"Let's do it," Jenga said.

Berner held up a restraining hand. "I have to know that both of you are one hundred percent on board with this experiment. I hope, but I don't know for sure, that by putting on the rings it doesn't announce our colony to the world. If I had more time, I would do it farther away."

"Why don't we?" I asked.

He glanced over at Ki'ichpanil as well. "My curiosity has got the better of me, I'm afraid. But if you understand the risks, we can cut the rings off right away."

Jenga took a deep breath. "I trust you. But we've got to get going."

"I wish I could go with you. I want to hear everything you learn while wearing the rings."

Berner took a scalpel and dipped it into a solution. Then, taking hold of my hand, he cut a perfect circle around my left ring finger. Blood dripped down my hand. He handed me a gold ring—the one that had belonged to Ki'ichpanil, because it was slightly smaller. I glanced over at Ki'ichpanil and her eyes were fixed on my hand. I slid the ring down my finger; the red blood ran down my palm to my wrist.

Then Berner sliced Jenga's hand too.

At first, I didn't feel anything. Then suddenly, I did. All of my senses were involved with what happened. I could feel everything around me. I could picture all the objects near me, in my mind; even the smells stood out to me. The best way to describe it was I was seeing the entire room in my mind—the people, Berner and Jenga, Ki'ichpanil, the cage, and all the things in the science lab.

"Jenga, is that you?" I said it telepathically to the image of Jenga.

The thought appeared in my mind: "Zee? Yes, it's me."

I couldn't see all his thoughts, and I knew he couldn't see all of my thoughts. I tried to enter his mind. But he was able to close it off to me.

"We can talk to each other," I said to Berner, my eyes wide. I glanced over to Ki'ichpanil. "If we gave her ring back, do you think I would be able to communicate my thoughts to her?"

Berner hummed. "It would be an interesting experiment, but not yet. We don't know what she might be able to do once she has a ring back."

I nodded. I stretched out my mind to areas farther away from me. But the farther I stretched, the darker the images became. But I could feel the presence of the aliens. Standing where I was in the room, I could have pointed in the direction of their Golden City, with perfect accuracy.

"This might not have been a good idea," I said. "I can sense the alien life forms—they are a long way off, but I can sense them. They can probably sense us too."

"I can too," Jenga said.

“Do you want to take them off?” Berner asked.

I shook my head. “We’re leaving the colony anyway. Let me keep it on. I’m curious too.”

I focused on Berner’s human presence in my mind. “Do you see Berner too?” I asked Jenga.

He nodded. “I don’t feel any other humans,” he said.

Using my mind, I created a kind of shadow that completely enveloped Berner’s form, and he doubled over, clutching his head. “Stop!” he shouted. But his cry was cut off as he was suddenly completely frozen in place. I released him immediately.

“Thank you,” Berner said. He was relieved.

“I couldn’t see or feel any other humans nearby. We must not be able to feel them because the dirt acts like a shield, just as we thought.”

Berner recovered quickly once I had released him. “You must let me know everything when you get back. Please don’t take unnecessary risks. If something goes wrong, cut them off right away.”

Both Jenga and I nodded. Berner handed us black leather gloves and we pulled them over our hands.

“This should be interesting,” Jenga said.

Jenga led me out of the tunnel and took me to the elevator that ascended to the surface. Only the remnants and some of the others willing to carry spoils left the hive. The rest of the colony waited.

“It’s been a long time since I’ve been above ground,” I said. I had become so accustomed living with the dull lights, I wondered what it would be like. I suddenly realized how much I had missed the view of the mountains, the trees, and the changing seasons. The need to leave the dirt overwhelmed me, and I unconsciously begged the elevator to move faster.

"Make sure you keep your eyes closed for a few seconds when we first exit, so your pupils can grow accustomed to the light."

After only a few moments, we exited onto the blackened earth. I took a deep breath, but the smell of dirt was all that greeted me.

My gaze rose to the forest that surrounded the blackened earth. The last of the Remnants were fading into the trees, and Jenga and I had to run to catch up with them.

"Haven't you ever been caught running over the landscape?" I asked.

"No, the aliens don't like to come here. I think they don't like dirt."

I understood what he meant. Through the power of the rings, I could feel the dead earth, and it was like having the taste of dirt in my mouth. It was uncomfortable. Instead, I focused on the sensations of the aliens far away. Again, I knew the direction of one of their cities.

"Have you ever seen one of their cities?" I asked Jenga as we ran.

We had just caught up to the tail end of the Remnants line. "Yes," he said. "I saw one from a distance. It was formidable."

"What was it like?"

"Golden," he said. I groaned. "And massive, with many towers reaching into the sky. Oh, and they float."

I was confused. "Float?"

"Or hover, whichever word works for you."

"I understand that, but why?"

"As far as I know, when the Cabras settled here, they arrived in massive ships for space travel. When the ships landed, they opened into the massive cities."

I thought about this for a moment. The alien's technology was indeed more than I could comprehend.

"So, about this transport?" I asked, changing the subject.

Chapter 5

ξ

The Ants Go to War

Jenga and I found Queen quickly. She was giving instructions in the center of the horde.

We stood on the edge of a cliff overlooking a road paved with concrete blocks.

The transport line, as Queen called it, was created to move food, human cattle, and sometimes Cabras.

"Will there be a lot of Cabras on the transport?" I asked Jenga telepathically.

"Sometimes there are," he replied. *"But the transports are mostly automated."*

I watched with fascination as twenty Remnant soldiers lined up, holding large round cannons on their shoulders.

"Make sure you don't fire until I give the command. It must be synchronous, or else the hits won't dislodge the transport from the magnetic line."

"What does she mean?" I asked Jenga.

"The transports run on a magnetized track. Those concrete blocks down there keep the transport moving and in place."

"How do we dislodge it?"

"You see how we are up here on the edge of the cliff, overlooking the tracks? This is because we have to fire the missile launchers at the second transport car. That causes a derailment, and

all the transport cars behind then dislodge."

"But why the second car?" I asked telepathically. I liked feeling connected with Jenga all the time.

"We used to hit the first, but the momentum of the remaining cars didn't create a full derailment for the rest of the transports. They just plowed through and kept moving."

"What should I do once the derailment happens?" I asked.

"Grab whatever you can carry and run back to the colony. The gruel is most important."

The ground started vibrating, and several rocks jolted loose from the side of the cliff.

With my mind, I reached out toward what was approaching. I could sense a Minotaur in the front of the transport.

The transport came into my field of vision; it was like a giant white snake. It hovered over the track and sped even faster than I had imagined. I had never seen anything move so quickly. There had to be at least twenty transport cars.

Queen raised her hand and the cannon shooters waited; their eyes fixated on their target, their fingers on the button, ready to push.

"Wait for it," Queen said. Jenga stood at her side, his handgun cocked and ready.

The transport whizzed toward us, and I felt the anticipation building in my body. I thought about Jenga, our naked bodies lying next to each other, the kiss of his lips, his skin; the adrenaline felt similar. I shook my head to bring me back to reality.

"Fire!" Queen yelled.

Small rockets burst out of the ends of the Remnants' missile launchers; they reached the second transport car and exploded into the sides of it.

The transport car was knocked off the track; it careened into the grassy field on the other side, flipping over.

As the second transport car left the track, it caused the first car to skid sideways, and it came to a stop perpendicular to the track. The next dozen transport cars also dislodged, following the second car into the field.

As Jenga had said, the rest of the cars continued streaming forward on the track. The Minotaurs must have created a fail-safe to make sure at least some of their products made it through if a transport was attacked.

But since the stalled first car sat perpendicular to the track, it created an effective barrier—the rest of the transport cars collided with it, causing them to derail.

Suddenly, all the Remnants were running toward the transport. Goods were spilled all over the ground, and people grabbed gunny sacks of food.

"*Where are you?*" I called out for Jenga telepathically.

"*At the front of the transport, freeing heifers from the third and fourth transport cars,*" Jenga replied.

In my mind, I sensed the Minotaur who had been driving the transport. The Overseer wasn't injured from the collision, and it was getting out of the train. I could see, in my mind, his presence moving toward Jenga.

"*Jenga, look out!*" I yelled at him in my mind.

"*Fuck!*" he said in his mind at the same time.

I started running toward him, pulling my dart gun from my back and loading it.

As I reached the front of the crash, I saw the Cabras. It had Queen in a force field, but Jenga wasn't under his thrall at all.

Jenga's gun was fixed on the alien, and he was unloading his entire clip into its body. As expected, it wasn't accomplishing anything. Even though their flesh didn't respond to gunshot wounds like ours did, each bullet, however, made the alien very angry, and each blow caused it to take a step back.

As I reached Jenga's side, I felt the presence of the Cabras and he felt mine.

"Now, you die," it said to me.

I placed the blowgun to my mouth. *"No, I don't think so!"* I shot the dart. It stuck into the monster's shoulder, and instantly the alien fell to the ground, unable to move.

Jenga smiled weakly at me. "Thanks," he said out loud.

As we walked toward the alien, I saw Queen stand up and yell. "Go! Run! Now!" she ordered.

"A minute," Jenga said.

"Catch up!" she said. "Don't wait! If it wakes up, it'll kill you." She took off with the rest of the free heifers and nucksa, all carrying as much foodstuffs as they could.

"It's still awake," Jenga observed. He pointed the handgun at the Minotaur's face. "Will that kill it?"

I shook my head. "They have a protective plate over all their major organs."

Jenga lowered the handgun until it was inches from the creature's upper chest. "How about here?"

"That won't kill it either."

He pulled the trigger and unloaded a second clip straight into the alien's protective shield. As I watched the Cabras's eyes, I could see it felt pain. But the gun couldn't kill it. Its hand flinched. I took another dart from my belt and jammed it into its body.

I reached toward the presence of the alien and spoke to it. *"Do you want to die?"* I asked it. I knew it understood me.

"You can't kill me; no human can kill me."

A few strange visions appeared in my head, and I wondered if the alien forgot to block me off from seeing its mind. A word came to mind, but I didn't know it, and I saw an image of a Minotaur, dressed in a white protective suit, butchering a human.

The human body was hung upside down, her eyes still alive, as the alien sliced her neck. Blood poured out of her body. A bit of her blood spurted onto the alien's gloved hand, and it quickly went and washed it. Then the vision ended.

"Cut off its head?" Jenga suggested.

I glanced over at Jenga and pulled my knife from my belt. *"But with this, I can slice off your head."*

Its eyes widened as it realized what I was going to do. *"But it won't kill me!"*

"But maybe it will permanently disable you!" My knife slid between the soft skin of the alien's chin, and a bluish liquid leaked on my hand. The alien made a clucking sound with its lips as I cut around its short neck and head. A single ball joint held its head to its body once the flesh was cut away.

"The cartilage around the bone is too strong for my knife," I said to Jenga. I tried to saw it, but it was like trying to cut rubber.

With the point, I jabbed the knife into the strong cartilage and then twisted it, while Jenga pulled his foot back and kicked the head as hard as he could. The ball joint snapped and dislodged, and the head flew a dozen feet away, bounced once, and then rolled to a stop.

In my mind, I could still sense the alien's life force. I went to the head and lifted it by the horns. There was no light of life in its eyes. But its body was beginning to come out of the paralysis.

The body stood up, but it could not tell direction; it tried to lash out, but it couldn't find either of us clearly; it only had a sense of where we were from the gold ring. Their brains must not be in their heads, I understood. They must also be behind the protective bone plate.

Jenga took my knife and efficiently cut the gold ring off the alien's finger. With the ring cut free, the feeling of the alien's life force disappeared from my mind.

"He is as good as dead now!" I said.

Jenga dropped the gold ring into his pocket and holstered his gun.

Exhilaration flooded my brain, and all I wanted to do was feel Jenga inside me. "Fuck me!" I whispered, grabbing his shirt and pulling him to me.

His lips pressed hard on mine, and he pushed me up against the turned-over transport car. My hands fumbled with his pants as I pulled them down and let them fall to his knees.

He pulled up my skirt, and I grabbed his cock and directed it to my rose, which was pulsating with desire.

Jenga lifted me by the thighs, and I directed his cock into my rose. I let out a deep sigh of relief as his cock slid in; it was a paradoxical feeling of firmness and softness at the same time. But the overwhelming feeling was one of being filled. His cock felt like it belonged there, and as he pushed deeper inside of me, the rubbing felt like he was scratching an itch I never knew I had.

As we passionately sucked on each other's lips, I felt myself building to a climax. He pushed in hard again, and immediately a feeling of pleasure ran through my body. I felt light-headed, and I groaned loudly as my rose contracted and released multiple times.

My moans were too much for Jenga, and he released himself into me. I felt a warmness fill me up. He moaned loudly, giving a final couple of thrusts before he loosened his grasp on me and my feet slid to the ground.

We stood next to the transport, breathing heavily.

"We must leave. More Cabras will be coming soon," Jenga said. "Tonight, we will celebrate our victory in the colony."

"I want to do that again," I said to him mischievously. He smiled at me as we readjusted our clothing and then turned and ran toward home.

Chapter 6

ξ

The Revenge

Music with a tribal beat pumped and I saw people dancing as Jenga and I descended the elevator. There was pulsating music, food, and a clear beverage, like water.

I glanced over at Jenga. "Vodka," he said.

"Huh?"

"Potato booze. We only bring it out after we have pillaged a transport. It'll make you feel really good!"

Nothing could make me feel as good as sex, I thought to myself.

As we reached the floor, Sashim handed Jenga and me each a cup of vodka. "Have a drink!" she said.

I handed the drink back to her; something was bothering me. It was the image the alien had shown me just before I cut off its head. "I need to speak to Berner," I said.

"You want me to come with you?" Jenga asked.

"No," I replied. "You stay, have fun; you deserve to party." I smiled at Sashim, who was already bobbing to the music.

He raised his glass to me before pounding back the drink.

"I'll catch up with you later, and maybe we can have some alone time again," I said.

He kissed me just before I left.

I pushed through the crowd as people danced and gyrated to

the music. Some were singing.

Reaching the science wing, I hoped Berner would be there.

He was, standing next to Ki'ichpanil. "Hey," I said.

He turned to face me.

"You don't want to party with everyone else?"

"Nah," he replied. "I have fun in different ways. What about you? You don't want to go and enjoy the spoils of war?"

I paused. "Something strange happened," I said.

"Yes?"

"We decapitated a Cabras. I used the paralysis dart on it and then cut off its head. It didn't die, but it lost control of its external senses."

"What do you mean?" he asked.

"The gold ring still allowed him to sense our presence and general location, but nothing else. However, once we cut off the gold ring, he basically became a lump of meat."

"That is interesting," he said. "Do you have the gold ring?"

"Jenga does," I said. "Also, I spoke to it. I told it I was going to kill it. And it understood what I was saying."

"That is interesting," he mused.

"But something else happened. When it told me I couldn't kill it, it let some information past the guard, and an image and a word appeared in my mind."

"A word?"

"Lymphocyte, I think—or maybe it was blood."

"And the image?"

"An alien butcher was draining blood from a human. He was in a specialized suit."

Berner repeated the word several times. Lost in thought, he went to his table, opened a drawer, and pulled out a thick book. He flipped through several pages and scanned his finger down the page.

"I know what lymphocytes are," he said. "They're specialized cells that live in our blood and fight infection. They make up our immune system. But why would the aliens be afraid of them?"

"Maybe they're dangerous to the aliens?"

"Well, lymphocytes are located in our blood, and aliens eat our flesh, which means the components of our blood enter their body systems already—unless..." He trailed off and flipped through his book.

"Unless what?"

"Unless they need to have their meat well done."

"Why would that make a difference?"

"Before the Cabras arrived, humans ate a lot of meat, more than we do now. We grew farms of bovine to feed our populations. However, some of those meats we had to cook very well before eating. One of those types of meat was pork, or pig. But we cooked it in order to kill worm larvae that could make us sick."

"So, we have worms in us that will make the aliens sick?"

"Not quite," Berner said. "The T-cells in our blood fight infection. Maybe the reason they don't kill us on the battlefield is because they can't have our blood on them—or worse, inside them."

I remembered the image of the Cabras washing the blood off its hands so quickly.

"Just let me talk through this for a moment," Berner said. "It could be as simple as different blood types."

"Huh?"

"If we gave a Cabras a transfusion of blood, they would die because their immune systems would attack ours, and maybe vice versa."

"So, we might be able to kill them?"

“We might be able to kill them.” His gaze turned to Ki’ichpanil. “We could try on her.”

I nodded and looked over at the Cabras. There was something different in her eyes. There was a spark of light. Her hands were clenching the bars that kept her a prisoner.

Just then, Jenga yelled at me telepathically and awoke my senses. Somehow, he had reached through the walls of dirt to communicate with me.

“Drones!” I said suddenly and loudly.

I turned to Berner. “The Cabras have found us!” I could sense a dozen alien life forms descending the elevator into our colony. There were already a hundred drones flying through the main hub, shooting darts.

The screams of our people could now be heard.

“Come with me,” Berner said, starting toward the exit.

“I’m going for Jenga!”

He nodded and disappeared down the tunnel. I turned away and ran toward Jenga. I could sense where he was. He was coming toward me.

The sounds of gunfire could be heard, and before I entered the hub, a crowd of fleeing humans rushed at me. I pressed myself firmly against the wall and tried to fight my way through the oppressive tide.

I could hear the drones humming and darts flying through the air.

I felt an arm encircle my waist. I turned and found Jenga holding me tight. “Come on!” he said.

We ran down the tunnel, back into the science wing. Ki’ichpanil was standing in her cage, her eyes alert for the first time. Even without her gold ring, she knew that the Minotaurs were coming to rescue her.

The humming of a drone caused both me and Jenga to turn. Jenga had his handgun drawn. He fired two shots at the hovercraft, missing it completely, then his gun clicked empty. He reloaded with a new clip, but before he could fire, a drone dart hit each of us. I felt the paralytic taking effect.

Five other drones appeared and circled us. I sensed the Minotaurs approaching.

I recognized the first Cabras that entered the room: Bejlae', Ki'ichpanil's father. He went straight to the cage and ripped it open. Ki'ichpanil rushed out and grasped him tightly. Then she came over to me and bent down, looking me closely in the eyes.

Because of the paralysis, I couldn't feel the kicks when they started. She pummeled me over and over and over again. Jenga watched it happen with fury in his eyes, unable to do anything about it.

"*Stop!*" an alien voice ordered. It was an alien bigger than Ki'ichpanil's father.

"*They both have anillos le óolo'*."

I didn't understand the word, but I knew it was speaking about the gold rings.

Ki'ichpanil and her father looked down at me.

The more powerful Minotaur spoke again. "*Bring them to the city*."

I reached out telepathically to Jenga. "Why don't they cut off the rings?"

"I don't know," he replied.

"*Look, they are talking to each other,*" the Cabras said in disbelief.

Part 5

The Golden City

Chapter 1

ξ

The Transport

Hundreds of us were captured.

The minotaur aliens loaded us onto a transport. As I looked around, I saw that most of the captured humans were nucksa and heifers. I wondered if they had even bothered to run. Most of the Remnants seemed to have disappeared into tunnels, safe—for now, at least.

The Minotaurs around us had closed themselves off, so I couldn't use the golden rings to speak with them. But I could feel them, like black spots floating in the eye of my mind.

Jenga sat hunched over on one side of me. His shoulders were slumped in defeat. On my other side sat Queen, who had been captured as well. The Cabras must have been aware of the differences in status because we were given our own transport car, whereas the heifers and nucksa were loaded in behind us.

Briefly, I hoped the Remnants would mount an assault and try to rescue us. But I knew they didn't have the time to get organized for such an attempt.

"You understand them when they talk," Jenga said to me suddenly, telepathically.

"Yes," I replied in the same manner.

"What are they going to do to us?"

"They're taking us to the Golden City. That's all I know."

I knew Bejlae' was not happy I was being taken away to the city. He had wanted to kill me. Ki'ichpanil kept trying to tug at his arm and tell him I understood their language and what they were saying. But he didn't care.

The larger Minotaur seemed to be a leader of their protective forces, and it refused to listen to Bejlae'. He had kept looking at me with what I thought was awe, or at the very least, curiosity.

Bejlae' had also fought to have our golden rings cut off, but the elder had refused to listen. According to their conversation, it was morally reprehensible to cut golden rings off, no matter who wore them. Bejlae' argued we had done it to him and his daughter. But the elder said it didn't matter, and that a ring could not be removed by force while the wearer was alive.

Bejlae' had a solution for that too.

Queen was losing her mind. The composure she demonstrated as the leader fled as she chewed her upper lip. I realized that she had always been a free born. Her now being caged reminded me of the woman who died in my corral.

"I knew it was fucking trouble," Queen said. Her breathing was ragged, and I feared she was going to start hyperventilating. "This is your fucking fault," she said to me.

"My fault?" I hissed at her. "Mert captured me. And you decided to keep the alien! I told them it was a bad idea."

Queen stood, but there was no escaping the transport car. There were no windows, just small holes in the wall, barely large enough to stick our fingers through. The hum of the electromagnetic transport was a hypnotic calming noise. Queen walked over to the door, which was sealed from the outside.

"Fucking let me out of here!" she yelled. She kicked the door with all her might, until she had worn herself out. She collapsed into a sobbing pile on the floor. I felt for her. She had been free her whole life. But even if I was used to confinement, I had no idea what was in store for us.

I placed my eye up to one of the holes and looked out. I could feel the wind as the transport sped along the tracks. And then I saw the city. It was massive. Like Jenga had said, it looked like it was floating a dozen feet above the ground.

The sun caught the sides of the buildings that stretched a hundred, two hundred, a thousand feet into the air, touching the sky. The tallest tower stood in the center of the city. It looked like it was made of solid gold, and at the pinnacle, two gold rings spun on each other's rims like an infinity symbol. I felt fear and awe, like I was looking at a god's home.

"I see the city," I told Jenga. "It's just as you said."

He half smiled, and then he spoke verbally to me. "We are going to our deaths, Zee."

I gulped.

"No one escapes the city once you go in."

Everything went dark—but only for a moment, and then it was light again, and I looked back through the peephole. We had entered the city. I saw streets and buildings, and Cabras; lots of Cabras. There were larger ones, smaller ones, and ones the same size as Bejlae'. They rode their golden chariots, powered by their gold rings. They stood in them like gods, with their chins jutting out from their chests.

The transport came to a stop. The door to our car whooshed open and cold air hit me. Standing on the ramp was the Cabras that had overruled Bejlae'. It was difficult to read its features, but he seemed harder, crueler, and in my mind, he was a much darker image than the others.

Queen charged at the alien. "Fucking Cabras!" she yelled.

The drone next to the alien zipped into motion and shot a dart at her, striking her in the chest. It didn't slow her down right away. She reached the elder and with her fingers tried to jump up and claw at its eyes. But the paralysis overcame her quickly, and she dropped to the floor.

A Reaper-bot approached. As I looked at it, I could see its image in my mind and in reality. It gave me an idea: would the gold rings allow me to control it? I reached out hesitantly with my mind. Suddenly I was looking at the world through the eyes of the droid. The elder watched with fascination.

Then I felt the power of the Reaper-bot slipping from my grasp. I fought the presence that was stealing it from me. But the elder chuckled as it ripped control from me. It was an interesting mental battle. I knew that it hadn't wrested control from me because it was stronger. It had won only because it knew what to do.

"*You cannot do that!*" he said in the alien tongue.

I watched in horror as the Reaper-bot picked up Queen and held her tightly in its grasp. Pulling her face up to its metallic face, it looked her in the eyes. It raised a hand so a finger was pointed at Queen's temple. Queen's eyes looked wild, and I could tell she was terrified.

The bolt shot out of the robotic finger, like a piston, striking her temple. Instantly, the spot in my mind that I knew was her disappeared. Her life force had fled her body.

"*Take the meat to the processor,*" the elder ordered, once again in the alien language. I wondered if it knew I understood.

Another alien the same size as the elder arrived. "*What do you want done with those two*?" it asked.

"*They must be gloved,*" the elder said. "*Shackle them as well.*"

The alien approached Jenga and me. In its hand was a black lace glove. Taking Jenga's hand first, the Cabras slid the glove over his hand. Immediately, I lost my connection to him. I watched as the glove molded itself around Jenga's fingers. His eyes widened at the loss of power. With his other hand, he tugged on the glove, but it wouldn't move. It was fused to his skin.

The alien grabbed my hand aggressively and slid it into the glove. It didn't feel like a fabric, but like another layer of skin. I lost my internal sight and telepathic ability as it molded itself to my hand. Everything seemed as it had been before I put on the ring, except that now I felt like a part of me was missing.

"Take them off the transport," the elder ordered. The droid moved behind us. I felt an electrical shock to my lower back, causing me to jump forward. Jenga also jumped.

We walked off the transport and down the ramp. The area in front of me reminded me of the corrals. The entire room was massive, and it had the same white marble as the hall by our corrals at the farm, with a subtle difference: there were bulges in the walls, like roots from a tree not entirely under the earth.

Ahead of us, the nucksa and heifers were being funneled toward airlock doors that opened and shut before and after each one. The room loud and echoey, and the heifers and nucksa jostled each other as they were led by the Reaper-bots.

Jenga and I had to also pass through an airlock door in single file. It hissed sharply as I entered, and a gust of warm air hit me, blowing my hair around my head. It was difficult to catch my breath, but the sensation only lasted a moment, and I was moved on as the droid appeared behind me.

Jenga entered next, and once again, there was an intense gust of air. The alien didn't come with us; it was just the three of us.

The corridor we entered was long and empty, except for wall-size screens spaced evenly on the wall. They played scenes of humans having their throats sliced on a tiled floor in a massive stadium. With each kill, the aliens in the stands would cheer. I was shocked because, though I was repulsed by the fact the aliens ate our flesh, this new information showing them as cruel disturbed me even more. I recalled the book I read on bullfighting. Was this karma for our mistreatment of animals from *before*?

Jenga's eyes held no emotion. But inside, I knew he was seething.

As he glanced at me, he said, "Fight hard."

I wasn't sure what he was talking about. But we stopped in front of a familiar-looking door, like those that led into my corral back at the farm.

The Reaper-bot jolted Jenga forward.

"No!" I shouted.

The door hissed open, and the droid motioned me to enter.

"No!" I said firmly, refusing to move.

The electric shock struck me again, but I refused to move.

"Fuck you!" Jenga yelled, and he pushed to get to my side, reaching and fighting. The droid held him back with one arm and jolted me with the other.

"Stop making so much noise," the droid said in a metallic-sounding voice. It spoke the Minotaur's language, so Jenga didn't understand it.

"Get in," the droid ordered me.

Still, I refused to move. They would have to kill me before I would leave Jenga's side.

"I will shock you again if you don't get in."

The intensity of the jolt was magnified, and the droid held

Jenga firmly away from me as bolts of electricity hit me. It alternated between different places on my body: my thighs, my neck, my breasts, my sides, then my thighs again. The pain coursed through me, and finally I collapsed in a soggy mess to the floor. The Reaper-bot kicked me through the door, which hissed shut behind me.

I ran to the door and pounded on it. "Let me out! Let me the fuck out! Jenga! Jenga!" I cried, but I couldn't hear anything.

Chapter 2

ξ

The Killing Stalls

The room was small, with a bench, a hole in the floor for shit and piss, and a door on the far end. The only thing that seemed different was the left sidewall. It was metallic and smooth, like black tile.

I'm not sure how long I was in the stall by myself because there were no windows to see outside. I was fed a couple of times a day, and I slept when I was tired.

After some days, the black metallic television screen flickered with light. On the screen, a deathly spectacle unfolded. I seemed to be interrupting an already-scheduled program.

I sat down on the bench, unable to take my eyes off the screen. The humans stepped onto the tiled floor of the arena willingly. But most never left the stoop where the door shut. Each butchering only took a few moments, and I wondered how many people were killed this way.

I chewed on the corners of my mouth as I watched a nucksa step into the arena from a door that opened in the wall. I thought I heard the faint hiss of the door closing behind him. Most of the Minotaurs cheers sounded like snorts and bellows of a horn, or like a kind of loud mooing.

The nucksa, probably a few years younger than me, crouched down next to the door, which had closed rapidly. The aliens' cheering had changed to ridicule at the nucksa's lack of evident courage. I could see his blue eyes through his long blond hair, which was unkempt and oily. He chewed on his lower lip as every camera in the arena focused on him. My screen showed a different angle every few seconds.

There was a brief moment when the screen flickered to show the flying drones. These were subtly different than the ones I had faced back in the tree, an event that felt like so long ago now. They were completely black. Two barrels protruded from the nose and propellers whirled on the top and bottom. I realized that it would be more difficult to use my knife to dispatch them.

I reached down and felt at my side. My knife was still sheathed at my belt, as were my blowgun and satchel containing the darts across my shoulders. Why had they let me keep these? I wondered. Briefly, I recalled that none of us had had our weapons taken. It was like they wanted us to fight.

But the nucksa in the ring stayed crouched along the wall. I could hear the volume of the crowd swell as one of the drones circled a rounded pillar in the arena and trained its gun on the nucksa. Then it flitted away, and the crowd groaned. Whoever was controlling the drones was doing it in such a way to build maximum tension and suspense. It circled the stadium again and trained the gun on the nucksa. The crowd quieted in anticipation as the drone fired a dart, which struck the nucksa in the back. The jolt of the shot caused the nucksa to jump up and run like a frightened deer. His shoulders were hunched over, and his gaze darted around. I felt the same helplessness he was feeling.

The dart did not tranquilize the nucksa; rather, it seemed to have given him added vigor. He ran and dodged throughout the arena like a madman. Until, after a brief chase—and to the bellows of the crowd as he managed to elude several darts—the nucksa collapsed on a diamond-shaped dais in the middle of the arena. A moment later, a door hissed open and a Cabras stepped into the arena. It wore the same clothing as other Minotaurs, but thick leather gloves covered its hands.

I recalled the picture of the butcher bleeding a human. The butcher hadn't wanted any human blood to get on its skin. The alien stepped up to the nucksa. His chest heaved as bursts of air escaped his lungs, but the muscles of his legs would not move. I screamed at him to move, but he could not hear me. The young man raised his hands in a feeble attempt to block the alien that stood twice as tall as him.

The Minotaur reached down, picked the boy up by his left foot, and held him upside down. The nucksa looked like a limp cloth. The alien circled the arena, holding up his victim so the crowds in the stadiums could cheer. With a strike of the blade in its other hand, it slit the carotid artery, and blood poured out of the human like a river. I was amazed at how quickly the blood drained from the body. But not a drop touched the alien.

The blood pooled on the floor, but the screen fixated on the nucksa's eyes. The eyes, which were once blue, almost icy, glossed and clouded over like a fog had settled on them. I knew he was dead. The crowd cheered, and the screen flickered off, leaving me in a darkened room, alone.

The blood. Our blood. I opened my satchel, and found several of the poison darts that tranquilized the aliens and humans. Unfortunately, I had only five left, after having given five to Berner to research. I hadn't spent much time considering how the darts worked, but each one had a small syringe connected to a needle. When the needle struck the skin, it compressed, releasing the poison into the target. If there was a way to open the syringe, I could change out the tranquilizer for my blood.

I tried to open the syringe by looking for a clip or button, but I couldn't find anything. I even tried to split it with my knife, but I couldn't. I knew a Minotaur could walk into the room at any moment. But still, I could not open the syringe. I managed to snap the needle off, leaving me with only four darts. I dropped the syringe to my bench and leaned back, holding the knife.

I began to pick with my knife at the glove covering the gold ring. I was intrigued because the white glove was visible on my hand, but each pick of the knife felt like I was cutting my own skin. But in my mind, I knew it wasn't my skin. So, I sliced around the gold ring with the tip of my knife.

Excruciating pain ran the length of my arm, but there was no blood. It wasn't my skin. Once I had cut the entire way around, I carefully rolled the glove back, exposing the ring. Immediately I sensed all the aliens, but I still could not sense Jenga.

Fear flooded through me. If I could sense the aliens, then they could also sense me. Quickly, I rolled the glove back over the ring, and once again, I was cut off from the ring's power.

As I picked up the syringe, I was struck with an idea. All aspects of the aliens' lives were controlled by their technology, even these darts. I wondered if the gold ring controlled them. But I knew I would have to risk exposing the ring again to find out.

Carefully, I rolled back the cut portion of the glove. I hoped the sensation of my shadow would just be one in many—or that the crowd outside was so focused on the butchering, they might not notice me at all.

I pressed the syringe against the gold ring. There was a click, and the syringe opened. Inside was a cylindrical space filled with liquid, which I immediately dumped out. I did the same with the three other syringes and then covered the ring again.

Taking my knife, I pricked the end of my finger. A sharp, momentary pain ran along the appendage and dripped blood into the cylindrical space; it took several times reopening the wound and massaging my finger from the bottom to the top to get enough blood. But once I was finished, I had four syringes full. I wasn't sure what would happen if my blood entered a Minotaur, but I hoped it would kill them quickly.

The screen flickered to life as I stuffed the darts back into the satchel. I glanced up at the screen, assuming I would see another nucksa entering the arena. Instead, to my dismay, Jenga stepped into view. My breathing shallowed, and I ran up to the screen and placed my hand on his image. I felt a brief moment of elation as I saw his gun. Maybe he could win? But the fleeting moment of hope disappeared as the screen scanned the stands of the stadium, and I saw the aliens crowding around with standing room only, yelling, screaming, shaking their fists, and knocking their horns.

The camera view returned to Jenga's face. I traced the form of his lips and wished I could kiss him again. He looked confident and unafraid. I hoped I would be able to face my death with the same fortitude.

The camera angle switched, and he was staring straight into the lens. I clenched my hands into fists. Come on, Jenga!

Chapter 3

ξ

The Roar

Jenga stood with his hand resting on the handgun at his side. He looked like a cat, ready to pounce on its prey. His dark eyes squinted and held steady. The crowd's boisterous grunts and bellows had shifted to very loud murmuring. This was a different kind of human.

The camera flashed to the stands, and the air of anticipation was evident as some Minotaurs shifted on their seats; others stepped from side to side and hoisted their leather suspender straps over their shoulders. The camera again focused on the drones, which were circling the arena.

There were three drones in the ring, and they crisscrossed and zigzagged around the air, always hovering six to ten feet off the ground. They would dodge in and out of the three stone pillars that rose up off the floor like ancient buildings, each at a different level. A person could jump from pillar to pillar, if they could get on one before a drone attacked them.

But still, Jenga waited. His breathing was regular, whereas mine was as rapid as my beating heart. His fingers did not twitch, but I knew he could draw the gun and fire it with deadly accuracy.

A drone flew around a pillar, soaring toward Jenga. As it turned the corner, I could see the gun target him. The crowd hushed just as there was a loud huff of air, and a dart was fired.

Jenga rolled to the ground with fluid form and jumped up five feet away, on his feet with his gun in hand. There were several loud shots, and I heard them through the wall. Each bullet struck the drone dead center. Electrical sparks shot out, and then it fell to the ground.

The other two drones didn't wait. They came at Jenga from opposite ends of the arena. But he had been anticipating this stratagem, and he was already moving between the pillars.

He found the shortest of the pillars and jumped up the six feet to its pinnacle. In the same motion, he ran and jumped to the next one, which was eight feet high, and then again to the third pillar, ten feet tall. Standing on the top, he didn't wait for the drones to find him. He fired his gun three times, and another drone dropped to the tiled floor with a rash of sparks and smoke. The third and final drone came up behind him and fired a dart. The crowd let out an audible roar as the dart skimmed past his shoulder and Jenga jumped back down to the floor. I saw him wince slightly as he landed.

But he moved so his back rested against the ten-foot-tall pillar, and he looked straight ahead. The drone would come from either the left side or the right side.

He waited with the handgun held in both hands, resting just in front of his chest. My heart raced as I waited with him. What would the aliens do if he destroyed all three drones? Would they let him live? Would they send more drones? He was bound to run out of bullets soon.

Minute after agonizing minute passed, and the screen kept shifting from the drone, which was proving indecisive as it would head one way. Jenga, with his ears attuned, would look in that direction, and the drone would reverse and come back the other way. The crowd was getting louder as the suspense rose.

The camera rested on Jenga's hand, the one with the covered

ring. It occurred to me that the Cabras had not considered the implications of covering our rings. The gloves made us invisible to their technology and their telepathy.

The drone made its move. It seemed to decide to fly rapidly past Jenga and then approach from a different angle. Jenga fired his gun but missed the target. The drone spun and released three darts in rapid succession. I would bet those darts were tranquilizers, and not the stimulant the nucksa got. Jenga was just able to dodge out of the way as the darts struck the pillar and dropped to the ground harmlessly.

Once again, Jenga was on the other side of the pillar from the drone, and it would have to attack from either side. The camera stayed on Jenga, and I watched as he checked his ammunition clip. My heart sank, and I wondered if the aliens understood he had only one bullet left.

"You have to attack," I yelled at the screen.

He seemed to have heard me. Because in a flurry of motion, he dodged among the pillars and the drone flew crisscross through the arena, hunting him. Until Jenga came up behind the drone, which tried to spin to meet him. But it was too late; the bullet struck it dead center, and it fell.

The crowd went silent. Jenga sheathed his handgun, and we both waited to see what would happen next.

After a moment, I heard a sound. It started as a low rumble, like an animal growling in its throat, but it increased in intensity and volume until it sounded like a hum, then a roar. One alien in the crowd gave such a loud bellow that the entire arena shook and all the Minotaurs fell silent.

A door opened and a very large Minotaur stepped into the arena. Muscles rippled over its arms, chest, legs, back, and neck. It stood at least twice as tall as Jenga. Its horns and bovine face were black, with beady dark eyes. A hoop was pierced through its nose. And when it snorted, it smiled with the deadly teeth of a carnivore. It held a butcher's knife.

Jenga drew his gun and then dropped it to the ground with a clatter. He pulled out his own hunting knife.

"No one wins in a knife fight," he had said.

But I couldn't think of any way the mammoth Cabras would lose.

The beast moved its blade in front of its chest in random motions. On its other arm and wrist was a leather protective shield; Jenga had no such protection.

With the arrival of the Minotaur warrior, the crowd had once again gone into a frenzy. And I knew why. The alien was going into a knife fight; it ran the risk of getting human blood on it. The crowd was in awe of their own kind willing to risk death to kill the human.

The two warriors circled each other, searching for weaknesses.

Jenga was the first to attack. But the Cabras dodged and blocked each of Jenga's strikes. Jenga stepped back to a defensive position. The alien waited. It kept snorting and snuffing at Jenga. Without warning, the Minotaur charged. Jenga had just a moment to spin out of the way. But the bull changed direction. Jenga had barely regained his footing before he was dodging again. There were three such attacks. Each time, Jenga got out of the way. But I could see his chest beginning to heave.

"No!" I shouted. The Minotaur was trying to wear him out. And it was working.

The alien went to charge again, but it stopped quickly, striking with its knife; it reached within Jenga's protective stance and sliced up his arm and chest. Because he was close enough to the alien, Jenga managed a counterstrike along the Minotaur's upper arm. But just as they were unaffected by bullets, so too it seemed they were unaffected by the knife wounds. We knew that a knife cut deep enough could decapitate them or take off an appendage. But Jenga's strike was barely a scratch.

I could feel the sobs starting in my gut, and I let a few escape my lips. They came out like a prayer with no words.

Jenga had backed up; the front of his shirt was wet with blood. "Rub it on the alien," I said. My voice croaked as I cried.

His wounded arm hung limply at his side while his strong arm held his knife ready. I could see in his eyes that he knew he was going to die. One more attack from the alien would finish him off.

"No," I cried with a muted sob. "Please." I could feel tears forming in my eyes, and I blinked them away rapidly.

Jenga looked up, and it was like his brown eyes were resting on me, looking directly into mine, just as they had when we first kissed in the hall. I couldn't hear it, but I read his lips. "I love you, Zee."

The weak sobs in my gut became a raging fire. "FUCK YOU, YOU MOTHER FUCKERS!" I yelled with everything in my being. I swear the Cabras in the arena heard me, for its head turned slightly to the side.

"I LOVE YOU, JENGA! I LOVE YOU, JENGA!" He heard me. He fucking heard me. I saw a smile appear on his face. It stayed there as the alien charged the final time.

Jenga raised his knife, but he had no chance. The Cabras bowled him over, and as Jenga stumbled to the ground, the alien's knife sliced him along the side of the neck and a fountain of blood spurted up like a geyser.

Somehow, the alien remained untouched by the blood as Jenga fell to the ground, a smile on his face.

My fear was gone. Instead, I clenched my teeth together so firmly my jaw hurt. My breathing regulated, but my fingernails dug into the palms of my hands at the sides of my legs.

Chapter 4

ξ

The Destruction Mechanism

I paced in my cell. I was going to be next. The screen remained turned on, and I saw a Reaper-bot spraying the arena clean of Jenga's blood. I turned my gaze away.

How had the Cabras prevented me from controlling the Reaper-bot? My mind went back to the moment on the transport when they killed Queen. I had been able to see the world through the eyes of the Reaper-bot. But the Cabras leader had wrested control of the bot back to himself. He had slid a wall between my mind and the Reaper-bot's computer. Could they make our brains stop working, so we die?

The thought was intriguing, and I wanted to experiment with it. But how could I, without being caught? *Did it matter if I was caught?* Since I would die soon in the arena anyway, I decided to roll up the glove again, past the gold ring on my finger.

As soon as I did, the images of the Minotaurs returned to my mind. It seemed that they didn't see me, as long as they weren't focusing on me.

Closing my eyes, I began to search their images. Most of the images I touched were spectators sitting in the stands above me. There was something I felt in them—there was anticipation. They were waiting for me to fight. They thought I was even stronger than Jenga.

The image I was in sensed my presence, and I backed off and moved to another one. I dug a little bit deeper. Then I saw it: I was the human who escaped a farm. I was the human who understood their language. I was a celebrity to them, a prize cow who bewildered them. They wanted to know what I would do.

I pulled away again. How could they know so much about me? I wasn't anything special. It was just me.

At the thought of Jenga, the rage returned. I would never love another like him. He was my first everything. But he was a warrior, and he died. What could I hope to do against the Cabras butcher? Jenga was a far better knife fighter than me.

I went to another image. Telepathically, I searched the mind of this Cabras, and then I saw it. In the depths of their brains was a vein. It pulsated, beating rhythmically. As I followed it, I saw it was connected to the gold rings. Because I was inside the Cabras's mind, I wondered if I could sever the vein. Reaching out with my mind, I severed the vein telepathically with my presence, and I felt the alien jolt in fear. Then it disappeared from my vision. If I had been watching it in real-time, it would have been frozen, as if by a force field. I felt it reach out with its mind, but it couldn't make me move.

I pulled away, and I briefly sensed relief in the alien as it recovered. I covered the ring with the glove to ensure the alien didn't find me as the one who severed their link. I had been able to freeze Berner just by reaching into his shadow. But I could sever the alien's links, if they weren't aware of my presence in time to protect themselves.

After a few minutes, curiosity got the better of me, and I uncovered the gold ring again. I sensed a shadow moving near me, just outside the door to my stall. I gently poked around the edges of the shadow, but I didn't want it to know what I was doing. It wasn't aware of me; it didn't even think I had the capability.

The door hissed open, and a Minotaur about the same size as Ki'ichpanil entered. I could tell that it was a full-grown alien, just shorter than the others.

"I'm here to check your body systems," the alien said. It knew I understood it.

I was going to win this battle; I would need to act now. I reached out with my mind, found the vein, and severed the Minotaur's link.

"Release me," it demanded. It was still able to move, and it stepped toward me.

I shook my head. Using my telepathy, I forced her to freeze.

"How do you know how to do this?" it asked me.

"I'm more intelligent than you think I am. We all are," I replied. I kept my gaze firmly fixed on the alien's eyes. *"Why don't you like our blood?"* I asked.

"You will die in the arena," it told me.

I smiled. *"That may be true. But right now, I have you, and I can tour your mind as much as I want. You will answer my questions if you don't want me to know all your darkest secrets."*

The alien nodded. *"We are allergic to your blood. It's like how you humans can be allergic to a bee sting; if you don't receive the proper injection immediately, you go into anaphylactic shock and die. For us, it is similar. We have only a moment before our immune system kills us from contact with human blood."*

I was confused. *"But why do you eat human flesh?"*

The Cabras responded. *"Your blood, when it is cooked, doesn't kill us but intoxicates us."*

"Does the blood harm your skin?"

"No," the alien replied. *"But we can't risk any contamination*

of our bodily fluids."

"What is the power of the rings?"

The Cabras would not respond. Very well. I went searching. I could feel the creature trying to resist me, but because I could keep the barrier in place, I was able to overpower her.

The information I was looking for wasn't hidden deep in their psyche. Everything was connected to the gold ring—both the ones on their fingers and the ones on the highest tower in the city. All of the gold rings in the city functioned together, like a circulatory system.

"The city is a living thing?" I asked the alien.

It unconsciously shook its head.

"It is." Veins of fluid, like blood, ran through the entire city. The Minotaurs had given life to their technology by infusing it with their own blood.

The alien tried to fight me. But I already knew the truth. Yes, they were a technologically superior species. They were bigger and stronger than us physically. But they were connected to a network, and they had become dependent on the network to connect with one another. As their technology had advanced, it had taken on more lifelike forms until it was actually a living and breathing system. And like all systems, it was susceptible to certain threats. My blood was the virus they couldn't fathom ever getting into their network.

"You go now!" I ordered the alien. *"I will fight when the door opens."* I folded the glove back over the ring, and immediately the Cabras's mind disappeared. I saw a palpable sense of relief wash over its face, and it backed out the door, which opened automatically for her. I thought about trying to figure the door out, but before I had a chance, the other door, the one leading from my stall into the arena, flashed open with a hiss. The roar of the crowd greeted my ears.

Chapter 5

ξ

The Death Strike

The sound of the crowd was a thousand blasts of a strong wind, pushing me, buffeting me side to side like I was a boat in a sea of storms. The sound was exhilarating. It was terrifying. I knew they had all arrived to see me.

Glancing upward, I could see the enormous stadium. There were hundreds of rows of seats, and anyone sitting in the top row would have been looking at me like I was an ant. Directly above my head were large black screens, showcasing the entire arena. Right now, the cameras were fixed on me.

The Minotaurs snorted and grunted with such volume I couldn't make out any of the words. It was just a cacophony of noise. Horned aliens stood in their seats, shaking their fists toward me, bellowing with mouths open so wide I could see down the throats of those lucky enough to get front row seats to my execution.

The pillars had changed. There was now only a single pillar, standing ten feet tall in the very center. I gulped, fighting to keep the tears in my eyes. Jenga's body hung by his feet. I tilted my head and clenched my teeth. They wanted to enrage me. Well, they had accomplished that, but I wouldn't let it blind me. I would give them a death that would make me worthy of his.

Standing around Jenga were three Minotaur elders. They were each almost three times as tall as me, and all I had were a few darts and a knife. Each of them held a blade of light in their hands. But that was their only weapon. They had no protective gear except the leather straps over their muscular shoulders, connecting to a leather belt with a leather loincloth. Their belts rested on their hairy hips and their goat legs were locked and ready to launch.

There would be no introduction. It had probably already happened before I entered. I ignored the door hissing shut behind me. But the act of locking me in the arena reinvigorated the crowd.

Three Cabras. I had to fight three of them. There were no drones. Just three of the aliens. If this was the first battle, what else did they have in store for me?

In my hand, I held my blowgun. One dart was loaded into the barrel. My hunting knife was sheathed at my side. I knew there wasn't much room for error. I had four darts. I couldn't miss.

My gaze stayed firmly fixed on the aliens, but I kept my senses on high alert around me. I would not let them spring some kind of trap.

I imagined that it looked like a standoff, with both sides examining their opponent, waiting for the clock to strike high noon.

I counted my breaths, trying to focus. With each count, I glanced at Jenga's figure. At his belt was his knife, and his handgun—but I knew it was out of ammunition.

The Cabras waited.

Cautiously, I took one step forward. They responded with a tensing of the muscles. A hundred thousand spectators were waiting, barely daring to breathe.

In my hand, I held my blowgun. In my other hand, I held a dart, ready to reload. I would have to be fast.

I took another step toward my opponents. They tensed again. They wanted me to bring the fight to them. They had to know about the blowgun. Bejlae' would have told them I could tranquilize them. Was that what they were waiting for?

I took another step forward. At the same moment, I brought the blowgun up to my lips with a spin of my hand. It was fast. It was fluid. They saw me step and they tensed. But they weren't ready for the blowgun.

A loud whisp of air sounded in the silent arena, and a blood dart escaped the gun and hit the Cabras closest to me.

It took two steps toward me, then he started to bellow. It was terror, like his blood was on fire. Everyone watched in horror, myself included, as the Minotaur's skin began to bubble like hot lava. It happened so fast. He was screaming, like a dying animal. His scream was cut short as his vocal cords swelled up, and a moment later, he exploded. Skin, guts, horns, eyes, muscle flew in all directions, no longer recognizable as anything but shreds.

The aliens in the arena stared at their comrade with gaping mouths. The stadium was silent, and I risked a look up into the stands. All of them had felt the Cabras explode. Their connection to one another through the rings meant they felt it. They hadn't just passively watched one of their own dying; they had experienced it with him.

They heard the sound of my blood dart loading into the blowgun. They bellowed as I released my second dart. But the two remaining aliens were ready, and they dove to the side. Their shoulders screeched along the tiled floor. One of them landed behind the pillar with Jenga's body acted as a shield. My dart struck the wall where it had been, and blood seeped out of the end—useless.

Now aware I possessed a weapon that could kill them, the aliens somehow made the arena start to shift under my feet, like there was an earthquake, but I maintained my balance as the two missing pillars rose up through the floor. They would give the aliens protection, but they would also provide me with protection.

I ran toward my death. There would be no defensive position. I reached the five-foot pillar and jumped. My fingertips grabbed the edge. In a single motion, I pulled myself to my feet. I could see one of the Cabras getting up from the floor. I blew another dart, and it struck the beast in the throat. He clutched at it with his fingers, ripping the dart out of its skin as if that would prevent my blood from entering his body.

I ignored the screams as I hopped from the shorter pillar to the next one, a foot higher. There, I crouched and loaded the blowgun with my final dart. The Minotaurs tried to keep Jenga's pillar between himself and me. Behind me, I heard the other one I had stuck, explode. I grinned a deathly smile. The crowd saw it because a close-up of my face was plastered on the screens above my head. They focused on my eyes, and I was taken aback by the ferocity I saw there.

"Mother fuckers!" I yelled. I stuck my middle finger up at the camera in front of me.

The crowd was on their feet yelling for my death. Clearly, they interpreted my middle finger as: *fuck you.* I waited for the final opponent to make his move.

He started running around the edge of the arena. He thought he was clever, but I wasn't going to waste my final shot on a moving target.

After completing a lap, he was once again behind the pillar hanging Jenga. It was too far away for me to jump to. But suddenly, the Cabras summited it instead. His massive form towered over me. His long arms could reach me from there.

He swung the blade in his hands, and as I dove off the side of the pillar, I blew on the gun. I had no choice. I had to risk the shot. But he jumped, and my dart missed his shoulder by the width of a hair. We landed simultaneously, and he charged toward me.

It was my turn to flee around the outer edge of the arena until there was a pillar between us again. But he kept coming. Like a crazed animal, I ran to the pillar hanging Jenga, and I stood next to his body. His head was next to my head.

The Cabras turned to face me. One hoof pawed at the tile. It lowered its horns and held its arms out like it was going to engulf me in its grasp. He launched forward. I just had time to slide to the ground as his head plowed into the pillar, causing it to crack.

Such a blow would keep him at bay only momentarily, but I used the opportunity. With my knife in hand, I slid the blade up behind the protective bone shield at the sternum. With the palm of my hand, I jammed it home. The blade slid up, under the protective plate, into whatever organs were housed there.

The crowd was still hollering, thinking their champion had won. But the bull stood up. Bluish blood dripped out of its mouth, and it staggered a few steps backward. Looking down at its chest, it pulled at the knife. A spurt of blue blood leaked out with the blade, and the beast stood there with a dumbfounded look on its face. A gasping noise escaped its throat, and it fell to its knees.

Standing up, I grasped Jenga's knife. With three quick jabs, I sliced around the muscles and cartilage of the neck. Then I knocked its head off its body with a round-house back kick.

Silence. I turned to face my Jenga, brought my hand up to his face, and cupped his cheeks. Standing on my tiptoes, I kissed his lips. Then I took his handgun and stuck it in my belt with his knife. I picked up my own blade and sheathed it. With my blowgun firmly clenched in my hands, I waited in the center of the arena.

There was no sound for a moment. Then I heard a bellow from the crowd. It was different. The tone shifted from one of derision to respect. Mother fuckers. They chanted the name Ki'ichpanil had given me—my pet name. Despite proving my intelligence, my strength, they still thought of me as a pet. A very lucky pet.

The pillars started to lower, including the one Jenga was hanging from. They disappeared into the tiled floor, leaving Jenga lying there. The body of the Cabras—and its head, a dozen feet away—was also left with me. Five doors into the arena opened up and Reaper-bots exited them. They formed a circle around me. There would be no escape. Their deadly red eyes fixed on me.

I slung the blowgun over my shoulders with my satchel. "This fucking ends today!" I yelled.

I peeled back my glove. The shadows of all the Minotaurs came to mind. I could feel their presences pressing in against me. The five blue shapes of the Reaper-bots also surrounded me. With my mind, I reached out and took control of them, so that I was looking through their eyes as well as my own. They turned in unison as I forced them to create a protective wall around me.

The aliens tried to wrest control. But I had learned quickly. As they came at me, I severed their links. The battle took place in my mind. I made one of the droids pick me up. In one arm, it held me, while with the other, it jumped and grabbed the top of the wall surrounding the arena. It pulled itself up, and we entered the stands.

The Minotaurs backed away from me. I could see their terror. They were afraid that I was going to kill them too. I heard confusion as they screamed in their minds.

And then I saw what I was looking for.

I used the Reaper-bots to clear a path through the Minotaurs up to a large bulging vein in one of the walls. The Reaper-bot grasped the vein and pulled it out of the wall. Tile shattered as it came loose. Taking my knife, I sliced along the vein, and bluish blood seeped out of it. Then turning the blade to my own wrist, I cut a horizontal line, and my own blood started to pour out. With all my remaining strength, I shoved my hand into the vein. I could feel the pressure and suction pull my blood out of me.

My gaze darkened. Bright flashes and black spots appeared in my vision, but I held on. Suddenly, I lost control of the Reaper-bot. But in that moment, a collective cry came from the mouths of all the Minotaurs. And then I realized I had no connection to the gold rings anymore. And if I didn't, they didn't.

I pulled my arm out of the vein. It was pulsating and bubbling. I sliced a length of leather fabric from my vest, exposing my belly, and I wrapped my wrist tightly.

The Minotaurs were frantic with fear as they fled the arena. They had no direction, no connection, and they all but ignored me sitting on the floor. They couldn't connect to the source of the gold rings.

Then the buildings began to bubble, and tile cracked and shattered. I heard the rumble of destruction as bits of glass tile landed around me. The Reaper-bots were dead and useless, with no one to control them, and no power of the rings to give them life. I stood up and walked out of the stadium. The Cabras I came across backed away from me, fear evident in their gaze.

The hovering city crumbled around us. With the power of their technology failing, whatever caused it to float was breaking down. Suddenly the city started to incline sharply until one edge hit the ground at a forty-five-degree angle. The crash caused more buildings to collapse, and rubble spilled into the streets. The loss of their technology did not kill the aliens. They fled the city in chaos as explosions rocked buildings. I fled with them.

Eventually, I found the edge of the city and crawled down the rubble to the earth. Behind me, I heard the collective dismay of the Minotaurs, as many didn't make it out of the city.

Suddenly a massive explosion erupted near the tower with the gold rings. The Minotaurs who hadn't escaped were vaporized instantly. The shock waves lifted me up and threw me a dozen yards away.

As I stood, a bit dazed, I brushed my clothes. *You fucking aliens deserve it*, I thought.

Jenga.

Part 6

The Acceptance

Chapter 1

ξ

The Abused

I found the magnetized track of the transport and followed it. After struggling through the land without water or food, I reached the blackened earth a few days later.

But the elevator going down into our hive had been destroyed, and the elevator shaft was filled in with dirt. Despair. Of course, they wouldn't be there anymore, not with the Minotaurs knowing the entrance into our underground city. I had given a great blow to their civilization, but I hadn't destroyed their capacity to recover from it. They would be back.

The shack was still standing, so I entered it. A lifetime ago I had been brought here, nothing more than an escaped pet. I sat on one of the two beds and let myself cry. The tears came down my face, cutting tracks in the dirt plastered there. Then from my gut came a howl. It was loud. It was long. It was an agony that no words could express.

"Zee?" a voice said.

My shoulders heaved as I opened my eyes and looked to the doorway. Standing there was Mert, wearing his military fatigues and boots. His gun rested on his hip.

"I saw you walk in here."

"He's gone," I said. "They killed him."

He nodded, not knowing what words to say.

"But I got them."

"You definitely did something," he said, walking over to sit down beside me. "We haven't seen a Cabras in days."

"They killed Queen, too," I said.

"I'm glad you escaped," he said. There wasn't even a hint of accusation. I looked up into his eyes. He saw me. He saw me as one of them, not a herder, not a pet, and not a heifer.

"Thank you."

"Come on; let me take you to the hive."

I wiped my face and nose. "It's still there?" I asked.

"Yeah, we just needed to make a new entrance. It's even deeper into the blackened earth."

I stood and followed him to the new entrance. It was so cleverly hidden that I didn't even see the lift until we were upon it.

"Who's in charge?" I asked as we descended.

"Sashim."

I smiled. That was good news. "How many survived?"

Mert's gaze dropped. "There were many taken. We are half as strong as we once were. After the Cabras came, we were very weakened, and then several other human tribes came and raided our supplies. We are going to have a long, hard winter."

As we reached the bottom, it was the same hive, but we came at it from a different angle, The streetlights were dimmer, and most of the windows in the underground buildings were dark. A wave of sadness once again washed over me as my gaze rested on the dais where I had first seen Jenga. I wouldn't be able to stay here, I realized.

"Come," he said, taking my hand. "Sashim will want to speak with you."

Most of the shops were empty, and very few people were

milling about. They were afraid. And they had every right to be.

We reached the leader's quarters. Sashim was speaking to one of the Remnants when we arrived. She turned at our intrusion, but as soon as she saw me, she came over to hug me.

"It's our blood," I told her. "Our blood kills them."

She nodded. "I am glad you are here." She was about to say something else when Berner came in.

His round face was beaming when he saw me. But the joy changed immediately when he read the sadness on my countenance. "Jenga?" he asked. I nodded. "I am sorry," he said.

"I got them for it," I replied. It sounded so fucking cheap.

"You can get them even more," he said slyly.

"What do you mean?"

He held up two darts.

I blinked at him stupidly. "You know what our blood does?" I asked. It was more a statement than a question.

"I know." His eyes smiled mischievously. "When we had Ki'ichpanil here, I took some of her blood regularly. After the incident with the transport, I started to experiment. When I realized our blood literally makes their blood boil, I started to create weapons with the same compound."

He dug into his pouch and pulled out bullets. "These are the masterpieces," he announced. "The tips are hardened and filled with human blood. You can fire them from a gun. Once these bullets enter the Cabras's body, the bullet breaks down and our blood enters their bloodstream, creating the same chemical reaction."

"So we can kill them?" I chuckled, reflecting on a conversation we'd had so long ago.

"We can kill them."

"Can I have those?" I asked. He nodded and handed them

over. After taking Jenga's handgun, I reloaded the clip with the blood bullets. "I can't stay," I announced. "There's something I have to do."

"Wait," Sashim said. "I still want to hear about what happened at the Cabras's city."

"It is rubble," I announced. "I know how we can destroy them, and we should pass that information to all the other human tribes we can. It won't be easy, but it is possible."

"Where are you going?" Mert asked. "I'm going with you."

I shook my head. "No, I'm going to the white-domed farm. I don't want you to risk yourself. There might still be Cabras there."

"Why go at all?" he asked me. "You need help."

"I'm going to free Seffie. I can't ask you to risk yourself."

"I'll at least cover you to the edges of the farm," he said. I nodded.

The translucent dome that protected the white-domed farm was missing. And as I approached, it was quiet. There were no Minotaurs I could see.

I found the white dome that had once been my corral, and as I approached the door, the airlock opened automatically. It still had power. The lights in the white-tiled hall were on. My footsteps echoed on the tile as I made my way to the door. If the Minotaurs had fled but left the heifers and nucksa in the corrals, they would have starved to death.

I touched the door, and it opened. I stepped into the corral. The door stayed open behind me. Huddled in the center of the room was the herd. My herd. Deborah stood at the front facing the door, facing me. Seffie was just behind her. I noticed that in her arms was a child. It was a few seasons old. Standing in the middle of the herd, surrounded by the women, was a bullaman.

But my gaze didn't stay on them for long. For standing next to the wall waiting was Bejlae'.

"I knew you would come back here," he said. *"Most of us have fled to another city. But I stayed. I knew you would come back."*

I couldn't reply to him. We no longer had the power of the rings. Mine, I kept firmly under the protectiveness of the glove.

"We will rebuild the city and the gold rings," he said. He took one step toward me. *"The farm's power doesn't come from the rings. It is mostly automated from power we set up on this planet."* He waved his hand toward the herd. *"The product is safe."*

I backed away from him, moving farther into the corral.

"You took my daughter and for that I am going to enjoy eating your flesh."

I knew he couldn't understand me, but I spoke anyway. "You might be able to rebuild and even restore the gold rings. But I have one too." I flicked my finger with the gold ring at him. "And we know how to kill you. It is only a matter of time before we take back what is ours!"

He ignored my incomprehensible language. He was about to say something else when a shape darkened the doorway of the corral. Glancing in that direction, I saw Ki'ichpanil. She looked at her father, then at me.

Bejlae' didn't wait a moment longer. With his daughter present, he decided to charge me. With a fluid motion Jenga would have been proud of, I pulled out the handgun and fired three rounds into Bejlae'. The impact stopped him in his tracks. He started to huff loudly, like he couldn't clear his throat—like he was choking on a bone. The capillaries in his skin started to boil, and he let out a scream so loud and terrible that the women in the herd scuffled restlessly. When he exploded, bits of him flew around the whole corral. The herd scattered but quickly huddled back together.

I turned the gun and pointed it at Ki'ichpanil. Part of me wanted to kill her because of what she was. But there was a part of me that remembered how she had cared for me. Loved me.

Lowering the gun, I instead motioned for her to run away. She looked at the guts of her father, a familiar look of anger crossed her face, and then she took off. When I heard the airlock open and close, I finally holstered my weapon. Berner would be happy to know his bullets had worked.

The bullaman stood in front of the women, like he was a sultan protecting his harem. I walked up to him unafraid. I watched his gaze shift from me to the place Bejlae' had just been standing.

"Seffie," I said, holding out my hand.

My friend stepped forward, out of the herd, holding her one-year-old on her hip.

"What's his name?" I asked.

She looked at me and shook her head. Deborah came and stood next to her and answered for her.

"I came back for you," I said. "Come with me. You don't have to stay here any longer. Come and live with me, with the free humans."

Seffie blinked at me before turning to look first at Deborah and then at the rest of the herd. "I cannot," she replied quietly.

"Yes, you can," I said. "They will take your son and they will kill him. And then they will eat his flesh. You must come with me. I'm here to save you, to take you away from here just as we always wanted."

Seffie shook her head. "It was what you always wanted," she said sadly. "But this is who I am. There is nothing for me out there."

She was terrified of life outside the corral. She didn't have the same dreams I had had. “It’s better to be free. There is nothing to fear,” I said.

“I won’t go with you.” She turned her back on me and walked into the herd. And the women surrounded her so I couldn’t see her anymore.

We accept the reality we know, and we allow fear of the unknown to impede our desire to change. But she would never understand that.

“I am sad for all of you,” I said. “But I will continue to fight for you. I will fight until every Cabras has fled our Earth. If you refuse to choose freedom, maybe your children will.”

I exited the corral. As I walked along, I opened every single corral door I could. I looked back as an airlock hissed open. A few curious faces were peeking around the edges of the doors, and I motioned to them. “Come with me,” I said.

Epilogue

ξ

The Insemination Cycle

I can hear the rapids roaring behind me. A breeze runs up alongside the river, and I shiver briefly as goose bumps run up my arm. The willow bushes next to me whisper the truth: I am alive.

Sitting cross-legged facing me is a small boy, about five years old. His face is round like mine with lips like mine in a stern expression. We have the same hair, except, his hair is black hair like his father's, black eyebrows too. But his eyes. Ah, yes, his eyes are also his father's: brown, soft, and caring.

"Mom," he says. His tone is always quizzical and curious. "Tell me again. Tell me again the story."

"Tomorrow, Jenga, tomorrow." I smile to myself; some parts of the story are just for me. I gently touch my lips and remember my first kiss.

We stand together, staring at the river brushing against the shore, slightly calmer than the rapids farther up. I clasp his hand tightly in mine. "Come on," I say. "Let's run!"

He lets out a squeal of joy, and we make a break for the trees. We don't have a regular path through the forest; we don't want to leave a solid trail because this is our home. We choose to live above ground where the smell of the forest, the freshness of the air, the soft mossy ground reminds me of freedom.

Jenga's favorite journey is to the river. And we go there

almost daily. He loves to hear my story and about his father, and I love to tell it to him.

I let him run faster than me, and it is only a short time before we reach a clearing with a massive tree in the center. The tree stretches high into the sky and its green leaves fill the sky like a cloud.

He is already climbing up, using the small grooves chiseled in a long time ago. I climb behind him, ready to catch him should he miss. But he never misses.

Reaching the branch and the fold, we both stop and stand, resting against the tree trunk. He reaches over and clasps my other hand. I can feel the rapid beating of his pulse. He glances up at me, and my heart breaks because he reminds me so much of his father.

"Mom, we continue to fight."

"Yes, Jenga, we do. We will fight so all of us will be free. And at least now, we have a fighting chance." I stare toward the area where the white-domed farm still lies. The aliens have moved back in. But they are no longer as dominant as they once were. And I hunt them still with Mert and other Remnants, whenever I get the chance. Jenga stays with Sashim in the hive during such incursions.

To them, the Minotaurs, I am the darkness that steals their lives. All humanity might not be free yet, but I do it for the children. The children of the Earth that was.

"I love you," he says. He plays with a gold ring on his finger, safely covered by a protective glove. It's how we remain hidden.

I follow him into the tree and I start singing:

"I see green on the trees and red roses too

They bloom in the spring, just like you do.

And I dream the dream of a beautiful world.

The clouds float by in billows of white,
The sun sets low with reds so bright.
And I dream the dream of a beautiful world.

Fat rain, drops from the sky,
The sun breaks through, clouds going by.
Friends greeting friends, 'Hey, how are you?'
Lovers embrace, 'I love you.'

Babies born, innocent and free;
Their lives lived long, healthily.
And I dream the dream of a beautiful world."

About the Author

C.R. Endacott wrote his first novel as a high school student. He is a teacher and for many years taught high school English and English literature. His passion is philosophy and the pursuit of knowledge and truth. He lives in Kamloops British Columbia, Canada with his wife and children.

Manufactured by Amazon.ca
Bolton, ON